FLOOD

was an Apache-trained bushwhacker who liked to kill like a rattlesnake from ambush and vanish like a ghost into the wilderness.

YARBOROUGH

was a mountain of a man who liked to use his awesome strength and professional fighter's skills to kill with his bare hands.

WHEELOCK

headed up an army of hired guns he used to cow an entire town and kill anyone crazy enough to defy him.

Clayburn knew he had to take on each one of these men, facing them in their own territory, playing them at their own games. Maybe he couldn't beat them all but he'd be damned if he wasn't going to try. . . .

THE MAN IN BLACK

Al Conroy

A DELL BOOK

Published by
DELL PUBLISHING CO., INC.
1 Dag Hammarskjold Plaza
New York, N.Y. 10017

ISBN: 0-440-15875-3

Printed in U.S.A.
Previous Dell Edition #5214
New Dell Edition
First printing—March 1979

1

HIDDEN IN THE SHADowed rock formations atop the ruins of the canyon's east wall, a gaunt-faced man with dark, hooded eyes sat against the base of a jagged stone pillar, patiently finishing his smoke while he waited. His name was Alex Flood. There was about him the quiet sureness of an inarticulate man who had found a means of expressing himself through making other men die.

There was no flesh to spare anywhere on his long, leathery figure. He could have been anywhere from thirty to forty-five. There was a peculiar ageless quality to him, as though he had never been young—and would never be old because the passing years only served to harden and toughen him.

He wore the nondescript clothes of a buffalo hunter, which he had once been. He had also been an Indian fighter—but it was a long time since he'd worked at either trade. Flood was a professional stalker and killer of men. Of a very special breed. There was no hand-gun strapped to his hip, which was unusual in this part of the country where most men sported one at least for show. There was only the 15-shot repeating rifle leaning against the stone spire beside him—and the Bowie knife in his belt sheath.

He was taking a last drag at his cigaret when he saw the first rising of dust in the distance.

Flood's habitual guarded, watchful expression did not change. But he held his breath for a time, keeping the cigaret smoke in his mouth until he was sure it was not just a stray wind stirring up a dust devil down there at the far end of the long canyon.

When he was sure, Flood slowly expelled the smoke and

crushed the cigaret stub in the dirt beside him. He picked up his rifle and levered a cartridge into the firing chamber with a smooth, almost leisurely movement. Then he waited, letting the tension build up inside him to just the necessary degree, and no further.

The cloud of dust grew nearer. Before long a stagecoach drawn by a team of four horses began to take shape within the dust it was raising. Flood got his feet under him and eased forward to the lip of a shale ledge. He stretched out on the ledge and rested the barrel of the rifle in a notch between two rocks. Cradling the stock between his cheek and shoulder, he lined up the sights on the nearing stagecoach.

It was, as he'd been told to expect, a brand-new one—its bright yellow wheels and scarlet-and-black body gleaming in the afternoon sunlight. That far away down there, it looked as small as a toy. There were two men up on the driver's box. All that Flood could make out about them at that distance was that the man riding beside the driver was dressed all in black and carried a carbine.

There were, Flood knew, no passengers inside the coach. This was not a regular run. The stage was fresh from the factory, being delivered to its buyer in Glory Hole.

It kept to the exact middle of the canyon floor as it approached—a sensible precaution. The canyon was very old, and the cliffs on either side had been crumbling away for hundreds of years. All that remained of either cliff was a jagged line of tortured rock formations, rising up from slopes of rock rubble and fallen boulders, topped by eroded buttes. There were many places along either side where armed riders could be waiting, unseen. By keeping his stage to the middle of the canyon, the driver made sure that, if an attack did materialize from the base of either cliff, he and the man beside him would have time to get ready before the attackers reached them.

This bothered Flood not at all. Following the nearing stagecoach with his rifle sights, he slid his finger across the trigger and then shifted aim to the team of horses. Carefully, he gauged the distance, the speed of the horses, the faint breeze.

The stage was almost directly across from him now. The noise of its passage echoed loudly in the confines of the canyon—the pounding of the horses' hooves and the rattling of the stay chains, the creaking of the wheels and springy layers of leather thoroughbrace slings under the coach. Flood drew a shallow breath, held it, and gently squeezed the trigger.

The roar of the rifle blasted in his ear and bounced back hollowly from the opposite cliff wall.

The near lead horse went down with a dying scream, dragging the other three horses to a stop and bringing the stagecoach to a skidding, jolting halt. By then Flood had already worked the lever and shifted aim to the near wheel horse. Coolly, he triggered off his second shot. It caught the animal in the head, toppling it over against its plunging, terrified teammate.

Working another cartridge into the rifle's chamber, Flood now gave some attention to the two men who had been up on the driver's seat. They had leaped down to the ground as the stage skidded to a halt. Now both of them were sprinting across the canyon floor in his direction, each carrying a carbine. The fact that neither was wasting ammunition trying to fire back at him indicated that they were not amateurs. There was no way they could hit him, firing from below. They were concentrating on reaching the bottom of the crumbling cliff so they could work their way up to his position.

Flood's instructions were to let the driver live, so he could get the stage to Glory Hole with the two remaining horses. But since there'd turned out to be *two* men, that meant he could get one of them and still leave one to take the stage the rest of the way.

There was no special reason for Flood to do so—except that the two men below presented small, fast-moving targets—an intriguing challenge to his marksmanship.

Both of the men were almost at the base of the cliff when Flood made his decision to try for one of them. The stage driver was a heavyset man whose short, thick legs were pumping as fast as they could go. But he had fallen some 15 yards behind the other man—the one dressed in black—

who was moving with the speed of a mountain cat, crouched low and zigzagging erratically as he came on.

Flood chose the slower target. He followed the stage driver in his sights, led him a bit, adjusted for the fact that he was aiming down from a height at a tricky angle—and fired. The bullet kicked up a gout of dirt just behind the running man. Continuing to follow him with his rifle sights, Flood made a finer allowance for the angle, led the runner by a fraction more—and fired again.

The bullet hit the stage driver in the side and bowled him off his feet. He hit the ground on one shoulder, rolled completely over, and immediately began dragging himself toward the nearest boulder, leaving his carbine behind.

Flood flicked a glance toward where he'd last seen the other one—the man in black.

He was no longer in sight. Which meant that he'd reached the rocks at the foot of the cliff below Flood, and could now begin working his way up under cover.

Flood didn't worry about this. He'd scouted the area carefully before settling down to wait. He knew what route the man would have to follow to reach his position—and exactly how long it would take. He had more than enough time left to finish the job he'd come to do, and get away.

The stage driver had disappeared behind the boulder he'd been dragging himself to. Out in the middle of the canyon the two live horses were trying vainly to free themselves from the dead ones attached to them by the tangled harness rig. Flood sighted on the stagecoach. There were eleven bullets left in his rifle. With a workmanlike precision, he began pumping all of them into the body of the coach, shifting aim a fraction after each shot.

Smashing eleven lead slugs into a stagecoach wouldn't put it out of commission. The barrage did what it was intended to do—ruin the paint job, punch holes through the woodwork, and tear up the leather seats inside. It was the kind of damage that could be patched easily enough; but the brand-new coach would never look quite so pretty again.

When he was finished with it, Flood sat back on his heels and thumbed 15 fresh loads in the rifle, getting it done with a swift, practiced ease that had no appearance of hurry about it. Part of his mind was automatically keeping track of the passage of the seconds. It was time for him to pull out. By now the man in black would have reached the long dry gully that was the only way to climb up to this point atop the cliff.

Carrying his reloaded rifle in both hands, Flood moved away from the ledge in a crouch. The rear of the cliff was as much of a crumbling ruin as the front, tumbling down into a maze of boulders, broken sandstone pillars, and narrow, twisting ravines. It was back down there that he had hidden his horse. Once mounted, he would be able to ride off the way he had come, leaving no trail anyone could follow.

But ingrained caution made Flood delay starting down from the clifftop just long enough to check on exactly how close the man in black was at this point. Moving silently to a massive shoulder of rock, he flattened himself against it and carefully tilted his head until he was able to peek around the corner, down into the long gully up which the other man would be climbing.

The gully was empty.

Flood stiffened, then looked around him quickly, sliding his finger across the trigger of his rifle. The man in black was nowhere in sight. Flood cursed himself silently for having underestimated an enemy. It was something he would never have done if the man coming after him had been an Indian. But it had been a long time since he had been stalked by someone with as much know-how as himself.

The gully was the only way up to the point from which he had been firing. Which meant that the man stalking him wasn't trying to reach that position. Instead, he was doing exactly what Flood himself would have done if he were the other man: he had figured out that Flood must have a horse waiting somewhere behind and far below him, since no horse could climb very high on that cliff. And there were a number of areas along the broken face of the cliff where a man could get through from inside the canyon. At this moment the man in black was almost certainly circling somewhere behind the cliff, trying to get between Flood and his waiting horse so he could catch him coming down toward it.

Flood realized now that he was going to have to ignore his instructions to leave a man alive to take the stage the rest of the way. Survival came first. If he couldn't get past the other man undetected, he was going to have to kill him.

All the years of survival by infinite wariness and cunning were back with Flood now as he began making his way through the outcroppings toward the rear of the clifftop. He no longer underestimated the enemy he was dealing with. He was figuring out exactly what *he* would be doing at this moment if he were the man in black.

Merged into the dark shadow between two boulders halfway down the rear of the cliff, the man in black sat on his heels thoughtfully studying the maze of stone and clay and rock below him. His name was Clayburn, and he was doing a methodical job of narrowing down the number of possible places where the sniper was likely to have left his horse.

He was a tall, lanky man with heavy, sloping shoulders. His lean, strong-boned face had a hard, sardonic quality to it. His wide-spaced eyes were green, and difficult to read. The hands holding the Winchester carbine ready across his knee were like the rest of him: weathered and capable-looking, the long fingers lean and powerful.

A gold cravat and the worn bone handle of the Colt holstered on his right hip were the only relieving touches against the uniform darkness of his clothing. Everything he wore was of good quality—the broadcloth trousers and the unornamented leather boots, the flat-crowned hat with its wide brim, the short, open frock coat and fine-spun linen shirt. Not the kind of outfit he'd have chosen for what he was doing right now. But he'd had no reason to expect anything like this.

Keeping crouched down, Clayburn turned in the dark shadow between the boulders and squinted upward, searching through the rock formations between him and the jagged, broken crest of the cliff. It had been more than a minute since the sound of the rifle firing up there had ceased.

There was a growing sense of danger with the silence, tensing Clayburn's insides and sharpening his hearing. He listened carefully as he slowly scanned the outcroppings and gullies above. It would be almost impossible for anyone to come down off that disintegrating clifftop without starting some stone rolling underfoot.

But though Clayburn watched and listened for some time, there was no sign or sound of the sniper.

He went on listening as he turned back to his study of the area below. The sniper's horse couldn't be hidden anywhere above him, because the slope became too steep and rugged from there on up. And it wouldn't be very far below, because the sniper would want his mount as close as possible when the time came to get out. Which meant that the horse was somewhere fairly near in the area below him.

Clayburn narrowed down the possibilities in that area to three places where a horse could be hidden. Almost directly below him was a cluster of boulders. More than one horse could be in there without his being able to see them.

Off to the right of the boulder cluster he could make out the shadowed opening of a pocket in the ground. It was wide enough to hold a horse; whether it was also deep enough to hide one, he could not determine from this angle.

Off in the other direction from the grouping of boulders was the entrance to a deep ravine. A horse could have been taken in and tethered there. But there was a heavy growth of bunch grass and mesquite in the ravine's mouth, and from this distance none of it looked as if it had been trampled.

Clayburn decided to try the boulders below first. Twisting his head around, he searched the rocks above again. He made a long, careful study of it, but still could not make out anyone moving up there. Which was peculiar enough to keep his nerves keyed taut as he started out from his shadowed hiding place.

He threaded his way through the rock formations in a low crouch, finger across the carbine's trigger, following a circuitous route that would give him cover all the way to the boulders below. He took each step with fine-honed caution, so as not to dislodge any of the loose shale underfoot. And every few steps he paused to look around him and above him with slitted eyes that were used to studying the distances and finding what didn't want to be found.

Finally he reached a position where he could see in

among the boulders and detect daylight on the other side of them. For a time he studied the shadows among them, until he was certain none of the shadows concealed a horse. Then he turned his attention to the mouth of the ravine off to the left.

He was a good deal closer to it now, and the mesquite and bunch grass there still didn't look as if it had been disturbed. Clayburn shifted his concentration to the ground pocket off to the right.

There was no way he could reach it from here without exposing himself for a stretch of about 15 feet—something Clayburn had no intention of doing. But there was a shallow, arid stone gully that twisted upward toward a protected ledge from which he should be able to see down into the pocket.

Crawling to a massive rock spur, he peered around it cautiously. Looking upward again, his green eyes slitted against the harsh slant of the sun. He scanned the rock formations between his position and the crest of the cliff. There was no sign of the sniper. Clayburn searched for anything that might mean the presence of a man up there—some faint stirring of dust, a shadow where there shouldn't be one, a glint of sunlight reflecting off metal. There was nothing.

Which meant one of two possibilities: the sniper might be staying up on top of the cliff, well hidden, waiting for a chance to pick off Clayburn if he exposed himself. Or else, in spite of Clayburn's surveillance, the sniper was managing to work his way down the rear of the cliff without being seen or heard.

If the latter was true, the sniper had to be someone with the stalking know-how of an Apache who'd lived long enough to learn all the tricks. Part of Clayburn's checkered life had been spent tracking parties of raiding Apaches for the army. The fact that he had survived the job meant there weren't many who could outstalk him. So if the sniper *was* coming down undetected, he was dealing with an extremely dangerous antagonist.

Clayburn allowed a spurt of fear to reach the control centers of his nervous system. Fear was a useful tool if controlled properly. It could keep a man alive. He used it now to make himself move with extra care, all his senses needle-sharp as he crawled under cover to the stone gully. When he reached it, he found that it was even shallower than he'd expected—about knee-deep. Clayburn stretched out on the ground and snaked into the arid, dusty gully. He moved himself along with just his elbows and toes, his body raised a scant inch off the bottom and the carbine held in front of him with both hands. The gully made a hairpin twist, went straight for a space, and made another sharp turn.

He was halfway to the second bend when a rifle blasted at him from a position less than a hundred yards behind him.

2

THE BULLET WHISPERED past the top of Clayburn's head and smacked against the stone side of the gully. It bounced back in the opposite direction, missing his spine by inches.

Clayburn dropped flat, pressing himself down against the bottom. The unseen rifle roared again. A lead slug slapped the rim of the gully just ahead of him and winged off at an angle. Clayburn stayed flat down, not moving a muscle. As long as he stayed that way he was safe. The sniper could not see him from where he was shooting—or neither of those bullets would have missed.

There was no longer any question about what he was up against. The sniper *had* managed to come down from the clifftop—more than halfway down—without being seen or heard. Also, if the sniper could not see him, there was only one way he could have spotted his position—by dust Clayburn had stirred up snaking through the gully. And he had stirred up very little of it. So the man he was dealing with *was* something special.

Seconds dragged by in silence. There were no more shots. Clayburn remained motionless for several seconds more. Then he rolled over on his back, the carbine held tight in his lean hands, ready in case the sniper appeared. But he didn't expect it, and it didn't happen. Nor was there any further sound—only an enormous silence.

Clayburn lay there on his back, eyes slitted against the sunglare as he swiftly considered the other things those two shots had told him. Without being able to see Clayburn, the sniper could not have expected to hit him, except on the chance one of the bullets might ricochet into him. A chance too slim to be worth the sniper's giving his own position away by firing the shots.

So the sniper had fired for the deliberate purpose of doing precisely that: to advertise his own position. There could be two alternative reasons for this.

If the sniper's horse were in the ground pocket Clayburn had been angling toward, then he was now between the sniper and his horse. In that case the only way the sniper could get past him to his mount would be by feinting him out of position. If Clayburn now tried to circle around behind the spot from which the two shots had been fired, the sniper would be able to slip through here and get to the ground pocket.

But it was also possible that the sniper wanted Clayburn to think along exactly this line, so that he would stay where he was, assuming the horse was in the pocket and not bothering to work his way closer to make sure. Which would give the sniper the time he'd need to manage the distance in the opposite direction to where his horse actually was—in the ravine.

The ground pocket or the ravine—Clayburn weighed the one possibility against the other. He was a man used to thinking his way into other men's minds. He tried now to think his way into the mind of the sniper—a man he had never even seen, about whom he knew nothing except that he was an unusually good rifle shot and an even more unusual stalker.

Flood squatted in the protection of a jumble of rock two-thirds of the way down the slope and watched the gully into which he'd fired. He waited with iron patience, holding down the edginess trying to rise inside him. In a hide-and-seek duel like this, that was what you did when each knew where the other was—you waited and watched. More often than not, it was the one who moved first who lost.

Seconds dragged into minutes. Flood continued to wait.

Then he saw it—a faint rising of dust farther along the gully. Not much; not enough for most men to have spotted. Flood's dark, hooded eyes watched it. The man down out of sight in the gully was moving away from him, in the same direction he'd been traveling the first time Flood had detected where he was.

The barely visible stirring of dust in the air reached a rock spur at the other end of the gully. And there it stopped.

Flood continued to watch and wait. Two full minutes went by. There was no more dust. Finally, Flood's gaunt, leathery face relaxed a bit. The place that the man in black had chosen to hole up was a perfect place to ambush him on his way to his horse. If his horse were in the ground pocket down in that direction. But it was not. It was inside the ravine, at the other end of the slope.

Flood raised up a little and turned away, threading off through the rock formations towards the ravine. He used every bit of cover along the way, keeping well down out of sight, his finger still resting lightly across the trigger of the rifle gripped in his hands. When he was about a hundred yards from the entrance to the ravine, he stopped, turned, and looked back.

Section by section, he surveyed the maze of rock between him and the gully into which he had fired the two shots. He took the time necessary to be certain that no one was moving after him through that area. Seeing nothing to indicate that anyone was, Flood turned back and studied the stretch between him and the entrance to the ravine.

The gully into which he had fired at the other man was far behind him. But it was within carbine range of the ravine's entrance. Which presented a problem.

He had ridden his horse into the ravine from the other end, which could not be seen from here. And he would ride it out the same way he'd come in. But there was no way he could reach the other end from here, except by going through the ravine. And to reach this end of the ravine, he'd have to cross an uncomfortably long stretch of ground where there was no cover. No matter how fast he moved, there would be six or seven seconds when he'd be out in the open.

And there was always a chance that the man in black would be looking in that direction during those seconds. Flood had no way of knowing how good a long-distance marksman the man was—but he did not intend to get careless about him again.

Flood raised his hooded eyes and searched for an alternative. He knew what he was looking for, and it didn't take him long to work it out. There was a circuitous route he could follow, up through the outcroppings where he'd be out of sight the whole way. It would take him very close to the top of one side of the ravine entrance.

From there all he would have to do was take one long jump to the lip of the ravine wall, and drop down out of sight inside the ravine. Even if the man in black happened to be looking his way when he made the jump, there would be no time for him to take accurate long-distance aim. A man would have to be very close, and actually aiming at the right spot before Flood make the jump, to hit him in the split-second he'd be in sight.

Satisfied, Flood began working his way upward, following the protected route that would take him to his objective. It was not an easy route to maneuver, and it took time to climb it without showing himself, falling, or starting a noisy stone slide. But when he got there, he saw that he had judged the distance pretty accurately from below.

The last piece of cover was an eroded sandstone pillar, and from there it was less than seven feet to the edge of the ravine top. Grasping the rifle securely in one hand, Flood bent at the knees, tensed, leaned forward—and jumped. As he'd expected, that single jump was all that was needed to get him across the short open space. His foot came down two inches from the edge.

He was bringing his other foot forward for the leap down into the ravine when a carbine shot sounded, no more than 50 yards away.

Flood heard the shot at the same time that the bullet thudded into the stock of his rifle and slammed it against the side of his chest with crushing force. The rifle spilled from his numbed hand as he toppled over the edge and fell straight down into the mesquite-choked ravine.

Hunkered down under a shale overhang some 50 yards from the ravine, halfway up the slope, Clayburn had been watching the ravine entrance when it happened. If he had had more time to study other possible approaches to the ravine, he might not have been caught off guard. But he had just reached the spot, and he wasn't at all sure that the sniper had actually headed this way. He hadn't found any sign of the sniper on the way here, not even a single bootheel print, though there'd been some stretches of dirt.

He had just settled down to watch the ravine entrance, still wondering if he'd made a mistake, when he caught the blur of movement higher up.

He twisted toward it instinctively, without any pause for thought, whipping up his carbine in the instant that the sniper's long jump got him to the edge of the ravine wall. There was no time for taking aim at any particular part of the man. He fired as soon as his sights lined up with the sniper's moving figure. And the next second the man was down out of sight inside the ravine.

Clayburn levered a fresh load into the carbine's chamber as he came to his feet. He didn't head directly toward the ravine's entrance—for the same reason that Flood hadn't. There was that long open stretch to cross in front of it, and the man inside might have a handgun—and be in condition to use it.

Instead, Clayburn climbed up through the outcroppings toward the spot where the sniper had jumped into view. When he got there the first thing he saw was the rifle, lying near the lip of the ravine wall with the bullet imbedded deep in its heavy stock.

Dropping to his knees beside it, holding his carbine ready, Clayburn cautiously leaned forward until he could see down inside the ravine.

The sniper was gone.

Even as Clayburn's eyes started searching for him, he heard the sound of a horse around a tight bend in the ravine, starting off in the opposite direction.

Clayburn's face took on a mildly disgusted look. Then one of his heavy, sloping shoulders moved in a sort of shrug. Picking up the fallen rifle, Clayburn rose to his feet and headed back across the cliff ruins toward the stagecoach.

He found Ben Greco—the man who'd been driving the stage—slumped on the ground leaning against the rock he'd dragged himself to after getting shot. Greco was a broad, bearlike man with thinning gray hair and the tough, broken-nosed face of an aging battler. Some of the battles he had lost, but not many. He'd been the best man Clayburn had ever seen with a handgun. Not the fastest draw, but once he had it out, he'd been beautiful to watch in action. And when Clayburn had first known Greco, all that bulk on him had been solid muscle. But he was getting old. And right now he looked even older.

His face was ashen and his eyes were squeezed shut against the pain. Both hands pressed a wadded bandana to his right side. The wad and the area of bullet-torn shirt around it were soaked with blood. His breathing was short and harsh through his clenched teeth.

Clayburn squatted beside him, put down the rifle and carbine, and spoke sharply: "Greco."

Greco's bloodshot eyes slitted open. "Took you a helluva long time to get the bastard," he grated without unclenching his teeth.

"I didn't get him. Let's have a look at that." He pulled Greco's hands away from the wound. The wadded bandana remained stuck to it.

Greco's eyes opened a little wider. "He slipped away before you reached him?"

"After I reached him."

Greco stared at him. "You must be losing your touch. When I was your age . . ."

"Shut up and lie down." Clayburn shoved him over on his side and examined the wound. The bullet had skidded along one of Greco's ribs, digging a deep trench from under his armpit to below the nipple. "Could be worse," he announced unemotionally. "The slug just tore about a pound of fat out of you and went on its way. At least we won't have to dig it out."

"I think my rib's cracked."

Clayburn nodded briefly. "Could be. Let's go." He got Greco's left arm across his shoulders and hauled him to his feet.

Greco weighed a ton, but he was able to take some of the weight on his own legs and help Clayburn get him to the stagecoach.

The coach looked like hell. There were splintered holes in the woodwork spaced from the front to the back, one of the lamps was smashed, and the leather of the rear luggage boot was sliced wide open. Inside it was just as bad. The paneling was ripped. There was a gaping hole clear through the folded jump seat. Another bullet had left a deep gash all the way across the high back of the rear seat.

Clayburn dumped Greco on the rear seat, unfolded the jump seat, and put Greco's legs up on it so he was in a reclining position. Getting one of the full canteens and a clean shirt from his saddlebags, he cleaned the wound and then tore up the shirt and made a tight bandage out of it to slow the bleeding. When he was finished, Greco lay back against the rear seat, his eyes closed, breathing a little easier.

Clayburn sat down on the front seat, facing him. "All right, Greco. Now tell me. What've you suckered me into?"

Greco put a hand to his bandaged side and let out a groan of agony.

Clayburn was not impressed. He'd once had to dig a slug out of Greco's shoulder. The slug had gone in deep, it had taken half an hour to cut it out, and there hadn't been any whiskey handy to ease Greco's pain. Greco had stayed conscious through the whole operation and hadn't made a sound.

"That wasn't any holdup attempt," Clayburn said flatly. "And that sniper left two of the horses alive. He wasn't even trying to stop this stage permanently. So it was done just to warn somebody about something, or to teach somebody a lesson. What somebody? The woman who owns this little stage line you've just bought a partnership in?"

"Maybe . . . ," Greco whispered without opening his eyes.

"Who's she having trouble with? And what kind of trouble?"

"I don't know . . . exactly."

"But you did know there was some kind of trouble.

That's why you talked me into coming along on this trip to spell you on the driving. Right?"

Greco opened his bloodshot eyes and glared at him. "For crissake, Clay . . . will you stop talking and get me to a doctor? I'm hurt, remember? You'll find out all about it when we get there."

"That where the trouble's coming from—Glory Hole?"

Greco nodded, groaned, and shut his eyes.

Clayburn looked at him without pleasure for several seconds longer. Then he sighed, got out of the coach and climbed up on the driver's box. Setting the brake, he climbed down and went to the horses.

Getting the harness rigging off the two dead ones was a job. Unhitching the live lead horse was simpler, but he had to hang onto the frightened animal to keep it from running away. He backed it up beside the remaining wheel horse and rehitched it in place there. Then he walked back across the canyon, gathered up the weapons he'd left behind, and carried them to the stage.

He tossed Greco's carbine and the sniper's rifle inside the coach, and looked at Greco lying there, pretending to be asleep. "Tell me something, Greco. Did this woman tell you there was trouble *before* you bought into the partnership?"

Greco nodded without opening his eyes.

"But you didn't bother to tell *me* . . . before I lent you all my poker winnings to help you swing it."

In spite of his pain, Greco almost managed a smile. "You might not've coughed up the dough."

"You know damn well I wouldn't have," Clayburn told him without heat. "You're a conniving sonuvabitch."

"Yeah. That's why we always got along. Two of a kind."

Clayburn slammed the door shut and climbed up onto the driver's seat, putting his carbine down beside him. With only two horses it would be slower going the rest of the way to Glory Hole; but they'd get there. And if that was where the trouble was, the odds were better than even that he and the sniper would be having another try at each other, sooner or later.

Taking up the reins, Clayburn released the foot brake and got the horses started.

3

GLORY HOLE WAS A sprawling town of adobe and wooden buildings in the notch of a pass that cut through the mountain range. The jail was a squat adobe structure on the north side of a small dirt plaza in the center of the old section of town. It was around this plaza that dozens of people from the town and the outlying small farms and ranches gathered that afternoon—to witness what they knew was about to happen. All of them hoping that something—someone—would stop it from happening.

They kept well away from the jailhouse itself, sticking to the buildings rimming the other three sides of the open square, hugging the walls up on the shaded boardwalks, watching from windows and doorways. None of them was armed. There was a town ruling that no one but law officers was allowed to carry weapons inside the limits of Glory Hole.

There was a single tree in the middle of the open square: a big, old oak tree. Three men stood waiting under its shade. All three were armed, though they weren't lawmen. The one leaning against the tree trunk and watching the jail—a stocky, mean-faced kid named Sims—wore two Colt revolvers in holsters tied down low on his thighs. The other two men faced in the opposite direction, watching the people crowding the other buildings; each wore a holstered gun, and held a double-barreled shotgun ready in his hands.

The three of them were gunmen working for Cole Wheelock. In the three weeks since the town's marshal had died trying to arrest Wheelock himself, no one had again challenged the right of any of Wheelock's men to ignore the law against carrying arms in Glory Hole. Certainly not the young, inexperienced deputy who was the only official lawman left in town: Jace Harcourt. Ever since the death of the marshal, young Harcourt had done his awkward, embarrassed best to maintain an appearance of doing his duty—while avoiding doing anything at all that might trip him into clashing with Wheelock.

But an hour ago something had happened that made it impossible for Deputy Harcourt to sidestep or back away any longer.

One of Wheelock's thugs had walked into a hardgoods store, picked up a couple boxes of cartridges, and started to walk out without paying. The storekeeper's wife had made the mistake of losing her temper and telling the thug what she thought of him. The thug had spun around and slapped her to the floor. It was more than the storekeeper could take. He'd snatched up a hammer, leaped at the thug from behind, and crushed his skull in. Then, knowing the fate of anyone who killed one of Wheelock's men, he had run to Deputy Harcourt, begging for protection and a fair trial.

He was in the jail now, with Harcourt. Both of them sweating it out; waiting, like everyone else around the plaza, for Wheelock to come.

When he did finally appear, there was a faint stirring among the people huddled along the boardwalks. Then there was an utter silence as they watched him with frightened fascination.

Cole Wheelock came walking out of the entrance to Water Street. He headed straight across the open square toward the jail—a big, powerful man with a wide, thin gash of a mouth and eyes the color of dirty ice. He walked, as he did everything, with a driving impatience that suggested an enormous store of violence locked tight inside him. There was an unstoppable look to him, like a glacier on the move.

Walking a few steps behind him was a short, slim, neatly-dressed gunfighter named Torrey, who acted as Wheelock's second-in-command in town. He was flanked by two other gunmen, each carrying a carbine in one hand and resting his other hand on the butt of his holstered Colt.

And behind them came Yarborough, a squat, solid bull of

a man who wore a gun like the others, but had never been seen to use it. His fists were his weapons, and he was rumored to have beaten several men to death with them. Bringing up the rear now, he carried an empty barrel in one hand. And in his other dangled a short length of rope, one end fashioned into a noose.

As Wheelock strode past the oak tree, the two gunmen with Torrey fanned out to either side of the jail. Wheelock kept going, not stopping until he reached the heavy timber door of the jailhouse. Then he looked back.

Torrey was standing a few yards behind him and to his right, his hand dangling carelessly near the gun strapped to his lean thigh. The bull-like Yarborough had stopped under the oak tree, upending the barrel on the ground. Climbing up on it, he tied one end of the rope around a thick branch over his head, with the noose end hanging down from it. When he was finished knotting the rope securely, he looked toward Wheelock and nodded.

Wheelock turned back to the door, pounding it with the side of his fist. "Harcourt!" he called through the small window in the door. "Open up. I want that man you've got in there."

Deputy Harcourt's face showed indistinctly on the inside of the small window. "You're not getting him, Wheelock." The young deputy's voice was slow and harsh with the effort it cost him to say the words. "He's my prisoner and—"

"He killed one of my men," Wheelock told him tonelessly. "Murdered him, without giving him a chance to defend himself."

"If he did or didn't, he's entitled to a fair trial."

"That'd be a waste of time. He's guilty. And you know it. I'm taking him off your hands."

There was a moment of silence. Then the deputy said: "No." The amount of nerve he had to work up to utter that single word could be heard in the way he said it—like a cry of defiance.

Wheelock stared at him expressionlessly through the small window. "You've got five seconds to open this door. If you don't, we toss dynamite in there and blow up you, him, and the whole damn jail."

The only answer was silence.

Wheelock waited—exactly five seconds. Then he looked over his shoulder. "Torrey, get the dyna——"

He was interrupted by the loud click of the jailhouse door being unlocked. As he turned back to it, the door swung open and Deputy Harcourt stepped out, carrying a sawed-off double-barreled shotgun trained point-blank on Wheelock's middle.

The deputy was a thin, wiry redhead with a young, freckled face. Young, and frightened, and determined. His finger was taut across both triggers of the sawed-off shotgun, holding its twin snouts inches from Wheelock's stomach.

Wheelock's eyes went down to the shotgun. Then, without a flicker of reaction, his eyes came up again to bore into Harcourt's.

"Boy," he said softly, "you drop that and get out of my way. Do it *right now*."

The muscles at the hinges of the deputy's jaws bunched into tight knots as his fear fought his stubbornness. "I know how fast you are," he said in a tight, shaky voice. "But even you can't get that gun out before I squeeze these triggers."

Wheelock continued to stare at him without expression. "You do that, boy—and a split-second later you'll be so full of lead it'll take four men to carry you to your grave. Look around, you fool."

Harcourt's eyes moved, just a little, taking in the gunmen in the square behind Wheelock: Torrey, the neat little gunfighter, watching him calmly from only a few yards away, his slim hand curled around the grip of his holstered Colt; the two with their carbines aimed at him, off to either side; Sims and Yarborough, in the shade of the tree. The only two not looking at him, ready to shoot him down, were the ones with the regular-length shotguns, facing in the opposite direction, watching the buildings and people on the other three sides of the square.

The deputy's eyes came back to Wheelock's. "It won't do you any good if they do kill me," he said thickly. "Because you'll be dead, too. Even if they kill me first, I'll still squeeze these triggers before I go down. It'll tear you in half!"

"That's right," Wheelock agreed flatly. "Then we'll *both* be dead. It's your choice. *Make it.*"

His eyes bored into Harcourt's. He began to bring his right hand up, very slowly, toward the shotgun whose double muzzles were almost touching his stomach.

Harcourt seemed frozen, unable to tear his eyes from Wheelock's.

Wheelock's palm reached the side of the short shotgun barrels, touched it—and paused.

Harcourt's throat worked convulsively.

Wheelock began slowly pushing the shotgun aside. The young deputy's nerve broke then, abruptly and completely. His hands went limp and his finger slid from the triggers. The shotgun was torn from him and thrown in the dirt. With the same hand, Wheelock seized the front of Harcourt's shirt, yanked him out of the doorway, and hurled him in the opposite direction.

Harcourt tripped and went down. He stayed down, on his knees, staring at the dust between them. His head sagging with the weight of his shame, feeling the eyes of all the people who had seen his cowardice nakedly exposed.

Torrey stepped over to him, bending down and taking the gun out of Harcourt's holster. The deputy didn't move. Torrey chuckled softly and his forefinger flicked the tin star on Harcourt's shirt. "Looks like it's too heavy for you, kid. Maybe I should tear it off?"

Wheelock's thin mouth smiled. "That would be disrespectful. He's still a deputy." He stepped back from the doorway and gestured at Torrey. "Bring him out."

Torrey hurried into the jailhouse.

A minute later a scrawny, balding man came stumbling out, his wrists handcuffed behind him, Torrey prodding his spine with Harcourt's gun. As he appeared, blinking into the sun, there was a sound from one of the people watching: a woman's scream.

The storekeeper's wife appeared from an alley and came running straight across the square toward her husband. Sims sprinted away from the tree and intercepted her, his foot shooting out and tripping her. She fell facedown in the dirt.

"Don't hurt her," Wheelock called out. "Just keep her quiet."

She was already trying to scramble to her feet. Sims shoved her down, pressing his knee into her back to hold her down, his hand clamping across her mouth to silence her.

The storekeeper appeared not to have noticed any of this. He stood there in the open with his face blank, staring straight ahead of him at nothing. As though, knowing he was going to die, he was trying to control himself by pretending that he was already dead.

Torrey prodded him forward toward the tree. The storekeeper's legs started to buckle. Wheelock motioned brusquely to one of the other gunmen, who hurried over and grabbed the storekeeper's arm, holding him up and marching him to the big oak. Wheelock followed them.

Yarborough was up on top of the barrel, waiting. When Torrey and the other gunman lifted the storekeeper off his feet, Yarborough reached down with one big hand and pulled him up, until they were both standing on the barrel. The storekeeper's eyes shut tightly as the noose was settled around his neck and drawn tight.

Yarborough jumped down off the barrel and joined the gunmen who had formed a loose ring around the tree, ready to deal with any attempt to stop this.

There was none.

Wheelock walked over to the barrel and looked up at the storekeeper. He spoke loudly enough to be heard by everyone watching: "You murdered a man. Now you've got to pay the usual penalty for murder."

The storekeeper's eyes opened and stared down at him. His mouth worked for a moment before the words came blurting out: "It wasn't murder! You're not the law! You can't just hang a man without a trial!"

"I *can,*" Wheelock told him.

"But he was hurting my wife! A man's got a right to defend his family!"

"If that's the way it was, you should have come straight to me and told me how it happened. I'd probably have understood. And forgiven you." Wheelock raised his voice to make sure no one failed to hear his words. "You went to the wrong place for protection. I'm the one who protects this place. You people have just got to get that through your heads."

As he said the last word, he raised his leg and kicked the barrel out from under the storekeeper's feet.

The man's drop stopped abruptly as the rope went taut and the noose jerked tight around his throat. He hung there twisting helplessly as he strangled, his legs kicking out uselessly, his face going dark.

When his movements finally ceased and he hung there, slowly turning in midair, Wheelock turned away and strode off across the square. One by one his men followed him, watching the buildings around the square as they went.

Wheelock went up Water Street and turned into Front Street. His headquarters was halfway up the block—a solid two-storey structure of adobe brick. He went in the open front door, into the saloon that took up the whole inside of the ground floor. There were only a few men at the bar. One of them was Flood, the new 15-shot repeating rifle that he had bought on his way into town leaning against the bar beside him.

Wheelock paused and looked at him. Flood moved his head in a single nod, to indicate that he had done what he had been sent out to do.

Wheelock moved on, up the curved stairway to the second floor. He went into the office next to his bedroom, and got a glass and bottle of whiskey from the sideboard. Filling the glass, he took a sip from it and then carried it over to the window. He stood there for a time, watching dusk settle in over the town.

His town.

4

THE LANG STAGE LINE'S office and waiting room were on the ground floor of a narrow two-storey building in the heart of Glory Hole. The top floor was taken up by two bedrooms and a washup room. Greco lay unconscious on one of the narrow bunks in one of these bedrooms, stripped to the waist. A doctor sat beside him, tending his wound by the yellowish light of an oil lamp on the room's single bureau.

Clayburn leaned against the wall and watched. The jolting of the stage-coach had started Greco's wound bleeding again, and he'd passed out sometime before reaching Glory Hole.

The doctor finished bandaging Greco, felt his forehead for a moment, and then took his pulse while observing his heavy, steady breathing. Finally he closed his bag and stood up.

"Doesn't seem to be any infection setting in," he told Clayburn. "I'll look in on him tomorrow sometime. He's weak from loss of blood, mostly. Let him have all the food and water he can take, and he should be on his feet again in a few days to a week, depending on his constitution. He seems to have a fairly strong one, considering his age."

Clayburn nodded. "He's not what he used to be, but he's still more than most. How much do I owe you?"

"Mrs. Lang said she'd take care of my fee." The doctor looked at the gun in Clayburn's holster, and the two carbines leaning against the bureau. "A bit of advice, Mr. Clayburn. There's a town ruling against carrying arms. It's enforced —rather brutally."

"Tough marshal?"

"We don't have a marshal any more," the doctor said. His voice was cautious, with a bitter undertone to it. "He's been dead three weeks. Got himself killed trying to make a man named Cole Wheelock give up his gun. They shot it out in front of Wheelock's saloon—fair fight. Marshal got his gun out, but that was all. Had two of Wheelock's slugs in him when he hit the ground, and he never got off even one shot. It's Wheelock that does any enforcing of town regulations now."

"I see. Thanks."

The doctor picked up his bag and went out. Clayburn gazed thoughtfully at the door for a moment, then at Greco asleep on the bunk. Then he unbuckled his gunbelt and put it on top of the bureau, next to Greco's. But he did not remove the slim-bladed knife concealed by his left sleeve, strapped to the inside of his left forearm in a soft buckskin sheath, with the flat hilt extending toward his wrist.

He went to the window and looked down at the night-shadowed wagonyard behind the building. It was bordered on two sides by a high wooden fence. On the other side was the stable into which Velma Lang had taken the two remaining team horses after fetching the doctor. There were two stagecoaches in the yard—an old, beat-up Concord, and the brand-new one that Clayburn had driven into Glory Hole.

Velma Lang came out of the stable and crossed the yard to the rear of the building with an easy, loose-jointed stride. A tall, strongly-built, and generously curved woman, she wore a man's shirt and boots, and Levi's held up by a wide belt buckled tight around her supple, narrow waist.

In her late twenties, she had obviously been around enough to know how to handle herself in most situations, without wasting time on unnecessary questions. After he'd brought the bullet-pierced stage in, she listened without comment to his brief accounting of what had happened. Then she had helped him get Greco upstairs, and gone running off for the doctor before he could tell her to.

She disappeared into the building below Clayburn. He stayed where he was, looking down at the two stagecoaches in the yard for a time. Then he turned and looked again at

Greco, making sure his breathing was still steady. Leaving the room, he went down the steps to the combination stage office and passenger-waiting room. Velma Lang was at the stove in the kitchen behind this room, getting the fire going under some coffee, beans and bacon.

Clayburn stood in the doorway, watching her. She turned her head and looked at him, without surprise. Her features were too strong for her to be called pretty. But her eyes had a startling quality that caught a man's attention instantly, and held it, if he could take their challenge. Long gray eyes, with a thoughtful appraisal in them that ignited a man's need. She was that kind of woman.

"Figured you'd be hungry," she said, after a moment.

He nodded.

She set out a plate, fork and spoon for him. Getting two cups and saucers, she put one down beside his plate, and the other across the table from it. Then she looked at him again. "You said you're a friend of Greco's. How close a friend?"

The corners of Clayburn's mouth pulled back in a kind of smile. "Come off it. You know. He'd have told you about me before he came down to Bisbee to borrow the rest of the stake he needed from me."

She smiled back at him. When she smiled that way, it accentuated the remarkable quality of those eyes of hers, and the boldness of her mouth. "All right—he told me. You're a professional gambler, and he thought if you were winning you might help him out. He said you used to work for Colonel Remsberg's Detective Agency, too. That you worked together for almost six months cleaning out a gang that was jayhawking gold shipments up in Montana."

She studied him for a moment. "I know Greco quit the Remsberg Agency because he figured he was getting too old for the job. Why did *you* quit?"

Clayburn shrugged. "I get restless, after a while." His green eyes looked into her gray ones. "*Mrs.* Lang . . . Is there a husband around here somewhere that goes with that 'Mrs.'?"

"There was. I'm a widow—twice. My first husband was a bartender in Cheyenne. Got killed by a drunk trailhand who was shooting at somebody else. The second one owned this two-bit stage line and broke mustangs on the side. One of them threw him headfirst against a fence post. That was two years back."

"Your husbands don't seem to have any luck."

Velma Lang went on meeting his eyes. "They thought different," she said coolly, "while they were alive to enjoy it."

She turned away and looked at the things on the stove. "Your meal's almost ready."

"Feed my curiosity first," he told her. "What've I got myself into? Who sent that sniper out to wait for us—and why?"

Velma glanced back to him, surprised. "Didn't Greco tell you?"

"No."

"I assumed he would have, if you were a good enough friend of his to give him the money he . . ."

"I didn't give it to him," Clayburn corrected her. "I lent it to him—at twenty percent interest."

"Oh. I see. That's the kind of friends you two are."

"I didn't lend him almost nine hundred dollars out of sentiment, if that's what you mean."

Velma filled his plate with the beans and bacon, and poured both cups full of coffee. Sitting down and picking up her cup with both hands, she began telling him between sips what he wanted to know.

Clayburn settled into the chair opposite her. He ate while she talked. And he showed no reaction to anything she said. But he listened attentively, considering each part of it, and filing various items away in the back of his mind for future use.

It started with a man named Lou Dixon, one of the biggest cattlemen in the county. Dixon had come into this part of the country with his cattle way back when there'd been no one there but Indians; built his ranch and spread out in a valley to the east of Glory Hole. There'd been no town at the time. That had come after a prospector struck gold in the neighborhood, and miners had begun flocking in. A few buildings had sprung up, and been named Glory Hole in honor of the first gold diggings.

The gold had petered out after only a few months, and

the miners had all moved on. But the town remained and began to slowly grow, because it was a natural stopping place for the freighters, buffalo hunters and immigrants following the pass through the mountains. Some of the immigrants reached Glory Hole and decided they'd gone far enough. They'd begun settling in, some opening businesses in town, others starting small ranches and farms outside the town.

It had been around that time that Velma's second husband had started his stage line. It hadn't been much—just a one-stagecoach affair. But between that and his broncbusting it had earned a living for him, and his wife, too, after he'd married Velma. With the town continuing to grow, and the traffic through the pass steadily increasing, he had been thinking of adding a second stagecoach to his line when he'd died.

It was shortly after Velma had become a widow that Dixon, the big rancher to the east of the town, had begun having trouble with the homesteaders spreading into the edges of land he considered his own by right of seniority. And when Dixon started accusing homesteaders and townspeople of rustling his cattle—which some of them were undoubtedly doing—relations between the big rancher and the town became increasingly strained.

Then, a year ago, something had happened that caused a suddenly spurt in both the growth of the town, and the stealing of Dixon's cattle: silver had been found in the mountains, north of Glory Hole. Once more the miners had flocked into the area. More saloons, gambling places, redlights and stores had sprung up on the outskirts of Glory Hole to service the needs of the miners. And large-scale rustlers had moved into the area to supply them with fresh meat in exchange for silver ore.

Dixon had done his best to fight the rustling and the encroachment of small ranchers and farmers onto his grazing lands. But there had been too many against him. Three of his line riders had been killed trying to trail rustlers. Dixon himself, tracking a man who'd killed and butchered one of his steers, had been ambushed and shot in the back. He'd survived, though crippled for life. And he'd seen the man who ambushed him—one of the small ranchers he'd been having trouble with.

Dixon had brought charges against the man, and come to the trial on crutches to testify against him. But the jury, made up of townsmen and homesteaders who considered Dixon their natural enemy, had found the man not guilty.

That had been the final straw for Dixon. He'd sent for Cole Wheelock, who was supposed to have run a big rustling operation of his own up in Wyoming, narrowly escaping hanging at the hands of vigilantes. The way the bitter Dixon felt, it took a thief to catch one. He had offered to pay Wheelock a regular income to protect his interests, put a stop to the rustling, and push the homesteaders back off land he considered his own. Wheelock had proceeded to do so—with the help of a hard-case bunch of gunmen, and an especially deadly character named Alex Flood.

"It was Flood that shot Greco and shot up my new stagecoach," Velma told Clayburn flatly.

He looked at her. "You sound sure of it."

"I am. It's the kind of job he does. Every time Flood disappears for a day or so, somebody gets found dead with a rifle bullet in him. The first one to die that way was the man who ambushed Dixon and crippled him. He was standing right beside his wife in broad daylight when the bullet got him, and his wife never saw a sign of the one who fired it. They say Flood was taken by Apaches when he was a kid and raised by them. He's like a spook. Even just walking through town. I've watched him. He merges into the shadows, kind of. Now you see him, now you don't."

Clayburn absorbed this while he washed down the last of his meal with the coffee. He leaned back in his chair and lit a cigaret. Exhaling, he squinted through the smoke at Velma and said, "All right, tell me the rest of it."

But he could guess the rest of it. He'd seen it happen before, in other places, when men like Wheelock and his crew were brought in for protection.

His guess turned out right. Wheelock had done the job Dixon had brought him in to do. Homesteaders had been pushed back behind a line set by Dixon; burned out, shot out or scared out if they tried to stay put. The rustlers had been cleaned out. Some had been killed by bullets fired by an unseen rifleman; others, in traps set for them by Wheelock and the rest of his gunmen. Others had been persuaded to join Wheelock, who began settling down and expanding his operations shortly after he'd proved he could protect Dixon's interests.

He was still being paid for protection; and he was also demanding that everyone else in the area pay him for similar protection—or "insurance," as he called it. Homesteaders who refused had their crops trampled and cattle taken by night riders. Town tradesmen who balked at forking over most of their profits had fights break out in their places of business—brawls that went on until they'd done enough damage to the place to drive home the need for Wheelock's protection. The last possible block to Wheelock's taking over the town had been eliminated when Wheelock had gunned the town marshal down three weeks back.

"No law at all left around here?" Clayburn asked.

"There's the marshal's kid deputy, Jace Harcourt," she told him negligently. "A brave enough kid—but green." Velma told him what had happened to the deputy that day, when he'd tried to prevent the lynching of the storekeeper. "Right now he's dead drunk up in his room at the Glover Hotel. Figure he'll stay that way a few days—till he sobers up enough to sneak out of town one night. He's too ashamed to ever look anybody in this town in the face again."

Clayburn chewed on that one for a time. "What about county and Federal law?"

Velma shrugged. "County sheriff's 90 miles away. He came once, but he didn't do anything. What the hell, Dixon's one of the biggest cattlemen in this county, and he's tied in tight with all the other big ones around. Those men stick together where things like rustlers and nesters are concerned, and they swing the most political weight in the county. If the sheriff went against them, he'd be out of office fast. And you know what that cattleman's lobby in Washington is like. Ain't no Federal marshal gonna come and interfere as long as Dixon figures he still needs Wheelock around."

"This Dixon is a fool," Clayburn said. "As soon as Wheelock has everything else sewed up, he'll turn on Dixon, too."

Velma nodded. "I told him that. But he's so mad at everyone else around here he won't listen. He's even let Wheelock have some of his own cattle, for a little spread Wheelock's started of his own. On land he scared a couple of homesteaders into giving up. I warned Dix the last time I was out to his place . . ."

She paused as she saw the way Clayburn's green eyes had narrowed on her.

"It sounds," he said quietly, "like you and this Dixon are kind of friendly."

"We are—but not like you mean. My husband started in this part of the country working for Dix, saddle-breaking wild mustangs for him. They got to be good friends—and I got included in the friendship when I married Lang. That's why I've gotten away with not paying insurance to Wheelock this long. I've been driving the one stagecoach myself—and Wheelock knows if he hurt me, Dix would turn on him."

Clayburn crushed out the stub of his cigaret and regarded Velma with a brooding look. "Uh-huh. Only around now Wheelock's beginning to toy with the notion he's maybe too big for Dixon to stop. And right at that same time you decide to expand your stageline."

Velma stared at him. "You put things together pretty quick, don't you? Well, you're right. There's new business to be had, carrying passengers and mail between the railroad down south and the mining camps north of here. But I needed two stagecoaches to handle it right, and I didn't have the money for another one. I went to the bank, but they wouldn't loan me that much unless I let the bank come in as a permanent partner. And while I was thinking that over, Wheelock heard about it and paid me a visit."

She got up and poured herself another cup of coffee, her face taut with remembered anger. Clayburn waited silently while she filled his cup, too, dropped back down in her chair, and looked at him again.

"Wheelock said," she told him, "that if I wanted my business to grow, I'd have to start paying him insurance, like everybody else. I told him to go to hell."

Clayburn sighed. "That was real smart of you."

Anger flared brighter in the depths of her gray eyes. "What was I *supposed* to do? Pay him? The cut he expects, I wouldn't be left with enough profit to make it worthwhile."

"Not pay him," Clayburn told her gently. "But not tell him right out that you weren't going to, either. All that did was make him keep tabs on you to check on what you were going to do about it. So he found out about your new partner . . . and your new stagecoach . . . and had this Flood waiting there to shoot them both full of holes. As a warning to you. Nice."

Velma spread her hands in a helpless gesture. "I'm sorry. I . . ."

"Why'd you pick Greco?" he cut in. "Because you decided if you had to let a partner in, he might as well be someone tough and experienced enough to have a chance against Wheelock?"

Velma nodded. "I once saw him clean up a town in Kansas, when he was still working for the Remsberg Agency. He was damned efficient about it. Then I ran into him again, a month ago, tending bar down in Salt Creek and not liking it much. So when I got to thinking about a partner, I went back down to see him. He was interested, only he couldn't work up enough cash to buy a new Concord. But he told me he just might be able to borrow the rest from this gambler friend of his—*you.*"

Clayburn scowled at her. "And you figured that if he could, you might wind up with *two* tough partners for the price of one."

"That did occur to me," she admitted coolly. She looked at him and shrugged. "Well, look at it this way. If I have to pay Wheelock, there won't be any profit left to pay anyone else. So if you ever hope to get your money back . . ."

"Oh, I intend to get it back," he told her with a small smile. "Plus the interest."

She tried to read his eyes, and failed. "You *do* understand there's only one way you'll be able to get it? Over Wheelock's dead body."

Clayburn's smile broadened. "You're quite a woman, Velma."

Surprisingly, the way he looked at her while he said it made her blush. Trying to hide it by taking a sip of coffee, she made a face and quickly put the cup down. "It's gone cold," she said, and got up. "I'll make a fresh pot while we're waiting."

Clayburn watched her go to the stove. "Waiting, you mean, for this Wheelock to pay us a visit about now."

Velma nodded. "That is what I mean."

They didn't have long to wait.

5

CLAYBURN WAS HAVING another look at the unconscious Greco when Velma called softly up the stairs: "They're coming . . ."

He moved before she'd finished saying the second word, turning down the oil lamp and plunging the room into darkness. Stepping to the bureau, he got the Colt from his holster. He carried it in his hand as he went out of the room and down the steps.

Velma was in the dark waiting room, standing back a bit from the front window so she wouldn't be seen. As Clayburn came over beside her she pointed. "That's Cole Wheelock in the middle. The one on his left is Torrey, Wheelock's chief lieutenant here in town. The one on the right is Alex Flood."

Clayburn looked through the window at the three men walking up the night-shadowed street toward the stage station. He looked first at the man on the right. He couldn't make out Flood's face, but that didn't matter. He wouldn't have been able to recognize it anyway. The brief glimpse he'd gotten of the sniper had shown him only that he was tall and thin. Flood fitted that.

The man in the middle wasn't so tall as Flood, but he loomed a lot larger. The man on his left, Torrey, appeared very small and insignificant beside him.

"Torrey," Clayburn mused softly. "Would that be Haggar Torrey?"

"Yes," Velma told him. "Why—you know him?"

"I know *about* him. Gunfighter . . . with twelve kills to his record, last I heard."

"He's improved on that record," Velma said bitterly,

...ere in Glory Hole. Two more—that I know about for sure."

The three men were almost directly across the street now. Wheelock and Torrey came on toward the stage station. Flood stayed behind, backing up onto the boardwalk on the other side of the street with his rifle tilted in the crook of his arm. Velma was right about him. He blended into the shadows. If you didn't know beforehand exactly where he was, you wouldn't notice him there.

Clayburn drifted back across the waiting room, into the kitchen. Out of sight there, he turned down the lamp and waited, the Colt dangling in his right hand.

There was a knock at the front door of the waiting room. After a moment, Velma turned up one of the wall lamps. Then she went to the door, unlocked and opened it. Torrey came in first, taking in the whole room with a single glance before backing off toward one corner of it. Wheelock stepped in after him, his powerful frame almost filling the doorway as he came through it.

"What do you want?" Velma demanded curtly.

Wheelock smiled down at her. "I hear your new stagecoach came in a short time ago—all shot up. What happened, a holdup?"

Velma glared at him. "It was no holdup."

"Whatever it was," he said with a tone of concern, "it's a damn shame it happened. Brand-new Concord, spoiled like that. It'll cost some, patching it up."

Velma just went on glaring at him, choking down the furious retort welling up inside her.

"You see, I was right," Wheelock went on amiably. "Your stageline does need protection. The insurance you buy from me is a guarantee against something like that ever happening again."

"Sure," Velma snarled, "in exchange for you getting a cut of my business that wouldn't leave me any profit left."

Wheelock shrugged. "It's better than going without protection, Mrs. Lang. What happened this time is bad enough. Next time it could be worse—if you know what I mean."

"I know goddam well what you mean!"

Inside the kitchen, Clayburn had been listening to Whee-

lock's tone. It was as he'd expected; they were not here for trouble. This was purely a business visit. Putting the Colt away on a cupboard shelf, Clayburn stepped out into the waiting room.

The two other men there stiffened as he appeared; then relaxed when they saw that he wasn't armed. Briefly, Clayburn took in Torrey—small, slim and dapper, his eyes calm and steady. Then he gave his attention to Wheelock.

Wheelock looked from him back to Velma. "Who's this—your new partner?"

Clayburn spoke before she could answer: "Yeah. And you're Cole Wheelock?"

Wheelock's peculiar cold eyes returned to him. "That's my name."

"Mrs. Lang's been telling me about you—that you want to sell us protection."

"If you think you need it," Wheelock said evenly. "Do you?"

Clayburn's face was carefully expressionless. "Judging by what happened today, it looks like we do. How much would your insurance cost us?"

"Depends on the size of the business you do," Wheelock told him. If he felt any sense of triumph, he didn't show it. He was still measuring Clayburn, taking his time about it. "Say 30 percent of what your stageline takes in, for a starter."

Clayburn ran a thumbnail slowly along the ridge of his jaw. His green eyes were dull, no trace of animation in them. "That's a lot," he said tonelessly.

"Uh-huh," Wheelock acknowledged calmly. "But you've got to weigh it against the chance of running into so much trouble that you wind up bankrupt."

"Thirty percent to you—that won't even leave us enough to operate on."

"We keep tab on your books. If I find it's cutting into your operating costs, you'll find I'm ready to lower my charges." Wheelock's mouth smiled. "After all, I don't want to put you out of business."

Clayburn asked with deliberate politeness, "Don't you think you ought to leave us some profits, too?"

Wheelock frowned slightly, sensing something hidden behind Clayburn's tone, but not quite able to detect what it was. "You've got to think of the future. Right now this part of the Territory's pretty lawless. But that'll change, in time. When it's finally law-abiding and peaceful around here, there won't be any need for my protection any more. Then I'll move on, and you'll be left with a going business. *Then* you can start making profits."

"That might be a long time to wait," Clayburn pointed out mildly.

"Yeah," Wheelock agreed. "It might. But you know the saying—better late, than *never*."

"You have a point there." Clayburn appeared to ponder it. "Give me some time to think it over . . . to talk it over some more with Mrs. Lang."

Wheelock shrugged. "Sure. She knows where to find me if you make up your minds. But remember—the longer you take, the more chance there is you'll run into more trouble."

With that, Wheelock turned on his heel and strode out.

Torrey drifted out after him. Clayburn shut the door and told Velma: "Quick—turn down that lamp."

The instant she did so, Clayburn sped up the steps to the room where Greco lay unconscious. Crossing the dark room in a crouch, he looked out the window, his slitted eyes studying the shadows beyond the back fence of the wagon-yard. After a few seconds he spotted what he was looking for. There was a man standing in the shadows out back there, holding a carbine, posted there to be ready, just in case there had been trouble inside.

The tall, gaunt figure of Flood appeared out there. He raised an arm and motioned. The other one went over to join Flood, and they strolled off together.

Clayburn straightened up, slowly. A deep crease had appeared between his eyes. This bunch Wheelock ran was careful, thorough, and well-organized. And there were a lot of them. It wasn't going to be easy.

He looked toward the bed where Greco lay and whispered, "Hurry up and get better, you sonuvabitch. I'm gonna need you."

The next morning, Greco was able to sit up in his bunk and eat the breakfast Velma had made him. Clayburn sat on the edge of the next bunk, watching him in silence until Greco finished the last of his coffee and sagged wearily against his pillows.

Clayburn took the cup from him and set it on the floor. Then he said, "Nice setup you've bought us into. Really beautiful. What's wrong with you, Greco—you getting senile or something?"

Greco's eyes looked at Clayburn, but they weren't quite in focus yet. "I'm getting old, that's for sure. That's why I had to quit Remsberg's Agency. Not up to all that day and night riding, catching my naps in the saddle. But I've tried some quiet, peaceful jobs since then—and they all bored me stiff. Hell, Clay . . . I may be getting old, but I'm not ready to spend the rest of my years just sitting around waiting to die of old age. So when Mrs. Lang come around with her proposition—"

"You jumped at a chance to die with your boots on," Clayburn finished it for him, with only a faint undertone of irritation. "And you figured *I* might as well, too."

"I wasn't looking forward to getting myself killed," Greco said weakly, "just to taking a few chances again. Unless you figure I'm *too* old, and don't have it in me anymore."

Clayburn looked at him for a moment. "No," he said slowly, "you're not that old. A professional like you never loses all of it. We both know that."

"Maybe not . . ." Greco whispered, and his eyes drooped shut. "I sure hope that's so . . ."

Clayburn watched him go back to sleep. Then he got up and went down the steps. Not finding Velma around, he went out and began prowling the town.

He strolled through Glory Hole for hours, wandering in and out of saloons, stores and other buildings. Until he had the layout of the streets and alleys and buildings—even the windows and doors—engraved in his mind. And he noted each Wheelock man he passed while he was at it. There were a lot of them, and they were easy to separate from other men. They were the only ones who wore arms.

Which gave Clayburn an idea—one that he tucked away with some others that had occurred to him.

It was past noon when he returned to the stage station. Velma was coming down the steps from Greco's room carrying a tray with plates and a cup on it when he came inside. She stopped at the bottom of the steps when she saw him. "Well, it's about time you got back. Where've you been?"

"Taking a walk," he told her.

She stared at him. "A *walk?*"

"Uh-huh. How's Greco?"

"Well enough to eat everything I made for him. The doc was here earlier. Said Greco's mending faster'n he'd expected."

Clayburn went into the kitchen. There was some hot coffee left in the pot. He poured it into a cup and sipped it as Velma came in. "I could use a meal myself about now," he told her.

"All right." She set down the tray and turned to him. "But there's something I've got to tell you first. There's going to be a meeting in Ed Ryan's dry-goods store down the street tonight. Secret meeting—some of the town's businessmen and homesteaders. That lynching yesterday shook them pretty bad. We're going to try to figure some way we can all act together against Wheelock."

Clayburn quirked an eyebrow at her. *"We?"*

Velma looked a little taken-aback. "Well—I thought *you'd* want to be there so—"

"I'm not going," he told her. "Neither are you."

Her mouth got a very tight look to it. "Oh?" she said quietly. "You're giving the orders around here now?"

He smiled at the ominous undertone in her voice. "Uh-huh."

"And what says I have to *take* your orders?"

Clayburn raised and lowered a shoulder carelessly. "You don't have to. But you were clever enough to latch onto two men who're professionals at handling this kind of trouble. I don't think you're about to turn stupid and go against what one of us tells you."

Velma looked at him for a time without speaking, studying him. Slowly the defiant set of her mouth softened. "All right," she said finally. "But do you mind at least telling me *why* we're not going to that meeting tonight?"

"Because it'll be a waste of time."

"Maybe not," she insisted, but she didn't sound sure of it.

Clayburn's smile was cynical. "It will be. A waste of time. And it might get us some new problems before we're set for them. All they're going to do at that meeting is *talk,* in circles. And not do anything afterwards. If they had the nerve to do anything, they'd have done it yesterday, and stopped that lynching. They didn't, and that means Wheelock's cut all the nerve out from under them."

"But maybe you could tell them . . ."

Clayburn shook his head back and forth slowly. "They're not ready. The way these things go, they won't be ready until something happens that gives them their nerve back."

Velma frowned at him. "Like what?"

Clayburn looked pointedly at the stove. "I'm getting hungrier every minute."

She turned to the stove, hesitated, and then looked back at him wonderingly. She was a woman who lived her own life her own way, and she was usually very sure of herself. It was something new for her to let somebody else do her thinking for her, and she wasn't quite sure why she was letting him do it so easily.

"But if we're not going to the meeting," she asked him, "what *are* we going to do? I'm not sending either of my stagecoaches out again until I know they'll get back in one piece."

"We're going to wait," he told her. "Wait and stall for time. Until Greco's ready to make himself useful again."

"And what then?"

Instead of answering, Clayburn asked her a question: "Know anybody who works at the hotel where the kid deputy's holed up with his liquor?"

"Yes." Her face was curious. "The man who owns the hotel, and his wife. They're friends of mine."

"Tell 'em to keep a check on the deputy. Let you know if he gets sober enough so he might make it out of town under his own steam."

"Why?"

"I don't want him getting away. We're going to need him."

Velma shook her head. "Jace Harcourt won't be of any use, drunk or sober. I told you. When Wheelock took the kid's prisoner away from him for that lynching, he broke the kid's spirit. Drained all the starch out of him."

"We'll stuff it back into him," Clayburn told her, "when the time comes."

Greco tried his legs after supper that night. Clayburn stood by the window and watched him shuffle from his bed to the far wall, leaning slightly to favor his wounded side. Moving slowly and carefully, he turned from the wall and came over to Clayburn. He looked out the window, breathing deeply of the night air. His deep-creased face was old and tired, but did not show any pain he felt.

With a faint sigh of irritation at his weakness, Greco lumbered away from the window, making the circuit of the room two more times before returning to his bunk. Lowering his bulk onto it in a sitting position with his bare feet planted apart on the floor, he wiped the sweat from his face and looked blankly at Clayburn.

"Shaky," he growled. "Shaky as hell. But that'll pass."

Clayburn nodded. "According to the doc, if you keep mending like you are, you ought to be able to ride in three, four more days."

Greco scowled. "You expect the opposition to just sit back and give us that long? Suppose they don't wait till I'm ready?"

"They'll wait," Clayburn said. "I'll manage it, one way or another. In the meantime, there'll be something *you* can do to make yourself useful."

Greco looked at him uncertainly. "I ain't gonna be up to doing a lot of moving around for a—"

"All you're gonna have to do is a lot of *talking*. You ought to be up to that pretty soon." Clayburn told him about the kid deputy, Jace Harcourt—and what he had in mind for him.

Greco listened thoughtfully to what he had to say. Finally, he grinned crookedly, "I taught you good, Clay."

Clayburn smiled. "I knew a few things before I ever met you, Greco."

"Oh, sure. But you still needed some lessons on the fine points."

"You were a good teacher," Clayburn conceded. "We'll find out if you still are."

"Depends if this deputy *wants* to be taught."

They discussed it for a time, going over every aspect of the situation in Glory Hole, assessing exactly what they were up against, drawing on experience to work out precisely what they were going to do about the size of the opposition.

When they were finished, Greco stretched out on his bunk to soak up more sleep. Clayburn sat on the edge of his bunk, smoking for awhile, carefully restudying every possible move and countermove in the game ahead. Then he got up and went out to prowl Glory Hole again and learn what it was like by night.

He spent some time wandering through the other side of town, where most of the activity was. What with all the freighters, cowhands, commercial travelers and buffalo hunters stopping over on their way through the pass, there was plenty of activity to observe. The saloons, red-lights and gambling places were all crowded and noisy, and the streets were filled with men in various stages of getting liquored up, moving from one type of entertainment to another. There were enough of Wheelock's gunmen in evidence, too, to make sure that the mass pleasure-seeking never erupted into the beginning of a riot. They were strategically placed where they would be able to handle any trouble that arose, breaking it up before it got out of control.

The last place he went to was the building Velma had told him was Wheelock's headquarters. He paused just outside the door, looking in over the batwings at the crowd inside while he considered going inside and joining one of the poker games. The saloon, which took up the whole ground floor of the building, was the best-guarded place in town. A man with a carbine sat in a chair at the top of the stairs, his ankles resting on the rail as he watched the activity below. In the saloon itself two gunmen wandered around keeping an eye on things. There was a sawed-off shotgun on prominent display behind the bar. And off in one corner sat Flood nursing a beer, a rifle leaning against the table beside him.

Clayburn chewed on the inside of his cheek as he studied Flood, and decided against going in. Turning away, he headed back through town to the stage station.

As he entered the darkened waiting room, he saw Velma standing there in the shadows, gazing through the front window into the street. Clayburn shut the door and came up beside her, looking in the same direction—toward Ryan's dry-goods store. "They holding the meeting in there now?"

She nodded slowly. "I still don't feel right about not being there. Ryan didn't say much when I told him I wasn't coming. But I could see what he was thinking—that it was because I'm too scared of Wheelock."

"That's as good a reason as any."

"But I'm *not* scared of him."

"You should be," Clayburn told her, and started to turn away.

Velma tensed suddenly, staring through the window. "Oh my God . . ."

Clayburn turned back to the window and saw what she was staring at.

Armed men were emerging from the shadows down at the far end of the street, coming straight on up the street toward Ryan's dry-goods store.

6

VELMA TWISTED AWAY from the window and tried to get past Clayburn.

His hand shot out and caught her wrist, stopping her. "Where d'you think you're going?"

She fought against his grip. "Let me go! Maybe I can slip in the back of the store and warn—"

"Too late," Clayburn said, not letting go of her. "The way Wheelock's men operate, there's bound to be more of them behind the store by now."

He looked out at the street again. Wheelock's men reached the front of the dry-goods store. There were nine of them, and they ranged themselves in a semicircle in front of the store, waiting.

Velma, finding she could not tear herself loose from Clayburn's hand, finally stopped trying. She stared at the men waiting in the street.

The door of the dry-goods store burst open and men began stumbling out—the unarmed men who'd been attending the supposedly secret meeting. Clayburn counted them as they came out. There were 15 of them. They came to a halt in the street, seeing Wheelock's gunmen blocking their escape.

Then another man came out of the store—Torrey. He stood on the boardwalk, gun in hand, looking at the cluster of frightened people caught in the semicircle of gunmen. He didn't say anything, just looked at them and waited.

A minute went by. Clayburn frowned. His grip on Velma's wrist tightened. "Any of the men who've come out Ryan?"

She looked at him, then back through the window. "No . . ."

At that moment another man emerged from the store—a squat, bull-like man.

"Who's that?" Clayburn asked Velma tightly.

"Yarborough. When Wheelock wants somebody hurt, short of killing, Yarborough's the one who does it."

Clayburn let go of her wrist. His hands tightened into fists, fingers digging into his palms. A savage sullenness had come into his face.

Torrey was gesturing at the unarmed men with his gun. "When're you people gonna learn?" he growled in a voice that carried down the street. "A town needs law and order. Conspiring to break the peace is a crime. The rest of you're getting off easy, this time. *Next* time—you won't. Now get out of here!"

The unarmed men immediately began slipping through the ring of gunmen, scattering toward their homes. When they were gone, Torrey and Yarborough started off up the street, followed by the rest of the gunmen.

Clayburn went out of the stage station as soon as they'd disappeared around a corner. He sprinted across the street, into the dry-goods store.

A man lay sprawled on his back in the middle of the floor, his face smashed and bleeding, his clothes torn, one of his arms bent at a terrible angle that meant it had to be broken.

Velma came running in behind Clayburn—and gasped sickly. "Ryan!"

"Get the doctor," Clayburn told her through his teeth. She twisted away and ran out the door.

Ryan's unconscious breathing was being done through his open mouth. His nose had been crushed. His front teeth were broken stumps. Through his ripped shirt livid, swelling bruises showed on his meager chest. Carefully and gently, Clayburn picked him up and carried him into the single large room behind the store. Stretching Ryan's limp figure out on the bed, he turned to a part of the room which served as a kitchen.

He had a large pot of water boiling on the stove by the time Velma got back with the doctor. Clayburn stepped back from the bed to let the doctor get to the beaten man.

His eyes had a dull sheen to their surfaces as he leaned against the wall, watching the doctor work.

Velma watched too, her face ugly. After a time she whispered, "Will he live?"

The doctor nodded without looking up, and went on with what he was doing. Clayburn went out into the store and lit a cigaret. He stood there, smoking and gazing out at the street.

Velma came into the store behind him. Her voice was tight with repressed rage: "What kind of man are you? To've just stood by and let something like this happen . . ."

He looked at her curiously. "What d'you think I should have done?"

"I don't know. You could have at least *tried* to stop it."

Clayburn shook his head. "I learned long ago not to risk my neck where there's nothing to be gained from it. I also learned not to get myself killed fighting other people's battles for them."

"You mean all you really care about is getting back the money you loaned Greco," Velma said scathingly. *"Plus* the interest, of course!"

She didn't see the faint flush of color that had risen to the taut flesh stretched over Clayburn's prominent cheekbones. His voice held no emotion at all when he spoke: "Sure. That's all. Listen—there were 16 men at this meeting, including Ryan. *They* could've stopped something like this from happening, if they'd really wanted to."

"They weren't armed! You know that."

"They could have been," Clayburn pointed out. "So could every man in this town be. Wheelock wouldn't stand a chance if this whole town was ready to shed some of its own blood to get rid of him."

"I'm not talking about the whole town," Velma snapped, too enraged to think about what he was saying. "I'm talking about one man named Ryan. I'm talking about a thug named Yarborough beating him half to death!"

"Yarborough will get paid for what he did tonight," Clayburn said tonelessly. "So will the rest of them—when the time comes."

He went out of the store and along the street to the stage station. Going through the waiting room to the kitchen, he turned up the lamp and took a large glass and a half-filled bottle of whiskey down from a shelf. He filled the glass, raised it to his lips, and drank until it was empty. Then he lowered the glass with a gasp, his eyes watering.

Velma came in as he refilled the glass. She started to say something. Then she saw the expression on his face, and shut her mouth without speaking.

Clayburn went on drinking until the bottle was empty. His eyes had a blurred look to them as he put it and the glass back on the shelf. There was another whiskey bottle there, a full one. Grabbing it by the neck, he carried it past Velma and out of the kitchen. The lines of his face had gone slack, but his step was steady.

Upstairs, he sat down on the edge of the bunk next to Greco's, put the bottle on the floor, and pulled off his boots. It took some doing. His fingers seemed to have swollen to twice their usual thickness. Uncorking the bottle, he stuck its mouth between his teeth and tilted it. When he lowered the bottle, it was one-quarter empty.

Clayburn stared blankly at the sleeping Greco. Raising the bottle, he drank again. Then he paused, appearing to be listening for something inside himself, before trying the bottle still another time.

When he paused the next time, he leaned forward with his elbows on his thighs, holding the bottle between his knees. Finally, he put the bottle on the floor, picked up his legs, and stretched them out on the bunk. Then he let himself fall back, and allowed his eyes to close. Almost immediately, he was swallowed up into a dark sleep.

By the time Velma came down to the kitchen the next morning Clayburn was already there, pouring himself a cup of coffee from the pot he'd boiled up. She stood there for a moment looking at him. His eyes were puffy and slitted against the hangover ache behind them. His lips were bloodless, and he choked down the first sips of coffee as if it were vile but necessary medicine.

Velma had been around enough to recognize when a man

was in no mood for conversation. Without a word, she went out back to tend to her stable chores, feed and water the horses. When she came back, Clayburn was on his third cup of coffee. His hangover was lifting, but not the savage need for a violent, explosive release of what had been building up inside him to the point of bursting. Having to go on bottling that need up inside him made his lean face a sullen mask.

As Velma went past him toward the stove she asked, "What do you want for breakfast?"

"I've had it." Clayburn's voice had a harsh rasp to it. He swallowed the last of his third cup of coffee and got up. "Where's the best place to buy a couple of riding horses?"

She told him, and eyed him curiously. "What do you need them for?"

Instead of answering he asked, "Where can I buy a couple of secondhand saddle rigs, cheap? I don't have much money left."

"You don't have to buy that. I've got extras in the stable."

"All right." He put on his hat and went out.

An hour later he came back, leading the two newly purchased horses. He put them in stalls next to Velma's riding horse and the stageline's team horses. Then he went across the wagonyard and into the kitchen.

He came to an abrupt halt just inside the rear door. Greco was seated at the table, finishing off a breakfast of eggs and bacon. And Velma was at the stove, fixing him a big second helping. Greco swallowed his last forkful of eggs and grinned at Clayburn. "Surprised?"

"You make it down the steps without help?"

Greco nodded. "Under my own steam. I'm still kind of weak, but the shakiness is gone. Just give me a little more time."

"Not much more," Clayburn told him. He lit a cigarette, smoking it as he watched the way Greco wolfed down the second helping Velma heaped on his plate.

When Greco was finished, he leaned back in his chair with a contented sigh, patting his heavy stomach. "You're a good cook, Mrs. Lang. If I had a few less years behind me

I'd be thinking about marrying you and sampling some of your other talents."

Velma gave him a quizzical look. "You might be disappointed."

Greco shook his head. "Uh-uh. I still got good eyes. You got the look of a woman just made to pleasure a man."

Velma laughed softly. "You're a lecherous old man."

"That's a fact," Greco admitted sadly. "I sure wish I was a lecherous *young* one again." He glanced at Clayburn. "Those looked like two good mounts you just took into the stable."

Clayburn nodded. "Come on out and have a closer look. You can pick the one you want."

Greco scowled at him. "You just want to see how good I can walk."

"That's right. Exercise'll do you good. Come on."

Greco placed his hands flat on the edge of the table and heaved his big, ungainly bulk upright. They went out across the wagonyard together, Greco walking with a slow but steady tread.

One of the horses Clayburn had bought was a buckskin, the other was a sorrel. Greco chose the bigger one, the buckskin. "Takes a lot of horse to carry all my weight any distance, Clay. But I sure hope you ain't planning on me doing much riding today. Or tomorrow, either."

"Not till you're ready," Clayburn told him.

They went back out of the stable. When they returned to the kitchen, Greco was breathing hard. "Think it's time for me to have another lie-down," he sighed, and trudged out into the waiting room.

Clayburn followed him as far as the inner doorway of the kitchen, and watched Greco climb the stairs. He had to cling to the bannister with one hand to help himself up, and his step was heavy and laborious, but he made it to the top without faltering.

When Clayburn turned back to face Velma the sullenness was gone from his face, replaced by a taut, calculating look.

"Time for you and me to go pay a call on that kid deputy now," he told her.

Deputy Jace Harcourt's room was on the second floor of the Glover Hotel, in the back facing an alley that divided the hotel from the rear of a restaurant. Velma unlocked the door with a duplicate key given to her by the owner. She stepped into the small, disordered room and wrinkled her nose with disgust as she saw Harcourt, passed out on his bed with one arm hanging down to the floor beside it.

Clayburn came in behind her. He studied the red-haired deputy's wiry figure and young, slack face; noted the empty liquor bottles scattered about.

Velma went over to the bed and looked down at the dark shadows under Jace Harcourt's closed eyes. "Emmy Glover told me he hasn't been out of this room once since the lynching. Sent down for what meals he had. And he only had two that she knows of. Left the tray outside the door, most of the food untouched."

Her voice did not reach through Harcourt's drunken stupor to his brain. He went on sleeping, breathing harshly through his open mouth.

Clayburn deliberately slammed the door shut. The noise it made had no more effect on the deputy than Velma's voice. He walked over to Harcourt and prodded him with his fingertips. The sprawled figure did not respond. Clayburn slapped the side of Harcourt's face. The deputy's head rolled with the slap, and he stirred a little, moving his legs and pulling his arm up from the floor. But his eyes did not open.

Clayburn looked to Velma. "It's gonna be a job. You get a bucket of cold water and a towel. Dump the water on him and work on his face with the towel till he comes around enough for you to pour coffee into him. Make the coffee hot and strong, and—"

"I *know* how to handle a drunk," Velma cut in shortly.

Clayburn smiled faintly. "Good for you. Like Greco said, you're a woman with a lot of talents. All right—from now on he's yours. Get him sobered up and get a meal in him. When he's fit to talk and listen, come let me know."

Velma frowned at him. "You're not going to help?"

Clayburn shook his head. "It's going to take a long time to pull him out of it. One of us should stay close to your place, and I figure it better be me. Wheelock's bound to be getting impatient. He just might decide to give us another nudge—to kind of remind us we still need the protection he's waiting to sell us."

"What do we do about it if he does?" she asked him pointedly.

Clayburn shrugged a shoulder. "Depends. We'll deal with it as it comes."

He went out, leaving her with Deputy Harcourt. As he left the hotel, he paused in front of one of the town notices he'd seen pinned up here and there throughout the town. It was the notice banning the carrying of weapons inside Glory Hole. It warned visitors to the town to leave their arms in their hotel rooms, or check them at the jail for safekeeping until they were ready to leave. According to what Velma had told him, Wheelock now had one of his own gunmen in charge at the jailhouse.

Clayburn continued to squint at the notice for a time, rubbing the knuckle of his thumb slowly along the side of his jaw. Finally he turned away and strolled back to the stage station.

Greco lay on his bunk having himself a nap, snoring softly. Without disturbing him, Clayburn got a pack of cards from his saddlebags and went down to the kitchen. Sitting at the table, he settled down to pass the waiting time playing solitaire, his long, rope-scarred fingers flicking out the cards with smooth, practiced precision.

He was still at it shortly after noon when Greco came thumping down the stairs to announce himself all slept out, feeling strong—and hungry again.

Clayburn made a meal for both of them. After they had eaten, they settled into a poker session, playing for matchsticks. The shadows of dusk were lengthening outside, and Clayburn had won most of Greco's matchsticks, when Velma came in, looking tired and irritable.

"Jace Harcourt's back among the living," she told Clayburn shortly. "He's sober, he's got food in him—and he's also talking about leaving town. I told you. He's got no intention of facing up to Wheelock ever again."

Clayburn scooped the cards together and stood up. He

stuck the pack in his hip pocket and put on his hat. "Give me five minutes," he told Greco. "Then you can show up and speak your piece."

Greco nodded, and watched Clayburn go out with a long, loose-jointed stride that ate up space without his appearing to be in a hurry.

Clayburn went straight to the Glover Hotel. He went up the stairs to Deputy Harcourt's door and opened it without knocking.

Harcourt was taking things from the bureau drawers and stuffing them into his saddlebags. He spun around at the sound of the door opening, his face going tight with fear. When he saw Clayburn, and realized he was not one of Wheelock's gang, the fright ebbed from him—to be replaced with an edgy anger.

"What the hell do you want?"

Clayburn closed the door and leaned against it. "The name's Clayburn. I guess Mrs. Lang told you I'd be around to see you."

"She told me," Harcourt said grudgingly. He looked awful, the way a man usually looked after a three-day drunk. A pounding headache wasn't doing anything to sweeten his disposition. "She said you were somebody new working for her. So?"

Clayburn smiled thinly. "I don't work for her. I invested in her business. Turns out I'm not likely to get my money back as long as Cole Wheelock's sitting on this town. So naturally I'm interested in dumping him off it."

"You can quit right there!" the deputy snapped. "I'm leaving—and I'm not interested in anything you've got to say about it!"

"How do you know you're not interested, until you've heard it?" Clayburn asked gently.

Deputy Harcourt didn't answer and did not meet Clayburn's eyes.

"Sit down and listen," Clayburn said. His voice was quiet, but there was a hard, relentless quality in it.

For a moment Harcourt seemed about to tell him to go to hell. But then he looked at Clayburn and changed his mind. He sat down stiffly on the edge of his bed, his fists clenching on his knees and his eyes fixed on the wall beside Clayburn.

"There's no point to this," he said in a low, shamed voice. "Whatever you've got in mind, I'm not the man that can help you."

"Yes, you are. You're the only legal law left around here."

"And I found out I wasn't up to the job. Wheelock proved that to me."

Clayburn's mouth thinned out in a grimace of impatience. "All he proved was that he's got more guns than you."

"No," Harcourt said bitterly, "he proved he's got more *guts*. I could have killed him—if I'd been willing to die, too, to do it. He was ready for that. I wasn't."

"You're pretty young. But you don't have to sound any younger than you are. Wheelock *knew* he wasn't going to die. Because he knew you weren't dumb enough to get yourself killed when there wasn't anything to be gained by it. That would have left the rest of his crew alive—and the storekeeper would still have wound up lynched."

Harcourt shook his head stubbornly, fighting against accepting anything that might indicate he was not the coward he'd convinced himself he was. "I was wearing a badge, dammit! And I failed to live up to what it—"

"You failed to stand up against overwhelming odds," Clayburn said in a faintly bored tone. "A man isn't expected to play hero just because he wears a badge."

"What the hell do *you* know about it?"

"Good question," Clayburn said lightly. "Well, for one thing, I used to work for the Remsberg Agency. Maybe you've heard about it?"

Harcourt looked at him, then, with a sudden dawning of respect. "Yeah . . . sure I've hear about it."

"I've been in things like this before. One thing I had to learn to stay alive is, you can't squash a crew like Wheelock's by yourself. You need the whole town behind you—with guns in their hands."

"That's just it," Harcourt said thickly. "The whole town was looking to me—waiting for me to do something that would give them the guts."

Clayburn eyed him gravely. "Sure. And getting yourself killed would have had just the opposite effect."

Harcourt chewed on that one for a moment. "But . . . I was supposed to do *something* . . ."

"Something," Clayburn agreed. "That doesn't mean something foolish."

There was a knock on the door. Clayburn opened it, and Greco lumbered in. He glanced from Clayburn to Harcourt, and back again.

Clayburn raised and lowered a shoulder slightly, and told Harcourt, "This is Ben Greco. He used to work for Colonel Remsberg, too. Matter of fact, he claims to've taught me everything I know."

There was a growing thoughtfulness on the young deputy's face as he watched Greco lower himself onto a chair with a faint wince. "How many more of you are there?"

Greco grinned at him. "Just the two of us. And you. That makes three."

"Three . . . ?" Harcourt's expression darkened again. "That's not enough to go up against all the gunfighters Wheelock's got."

"Spoken like a real amateur," Greco told him cheerfully.

Harcourt blinked, not quite sure if he was being insulted. "What's that mean?"

"Be glad to tell you, son," Greco said. "The difference between a professional and an amateur is just this: a professional figures out ways to cut down the odds against him before making his move. Now, me and Clay there—we're professionals. And you, boy—you are about to become the beneficiary of our experience."

Deputy Harcourt stared at the heavy old man, confused and fascinated. Clayburn decided that he was no longer needed. If anyone could make Harcourt see the light—which was still doubtful—Greco was the kind of spellbinder who could do it.

Opening the door, Clayburn slipped out and shut it softly behind him. Going down the steps and out of the hotel, he headed back through the dusk-shadowed streets to the stage station.

Velma was in the kitchen having herself a cup of coffee when he came in. She looked up at him sharply, the unasked question plain in her face.

"It's touch and go," he told her. "We'll soon know."

"Suppose Jace Harcourt *doesn't* come in with us?" she asked him. "What then?"

"Then we'll just have to handle it another way. But it'll be a helluva lot easier *with* him." Clayburn got a cup and filled it from the coffeepot. Sitting down across the table from her, he asked, "How long a ride is it out to Dixon's ranch?"

"Six, seven hours . . . why?"

"Our next move'll be for you and me to go out and have a talk with Dixon . . . see if we can turn him against Wheelock."

"It's worth trying, I guess," Velma said dubiously. "But I tried it a couple times myself, and it didn't work. I'm afraid it'll be a waste of time."

"No," Clayburn said, "it won't be that. We'll at least plant a couple seeds of doubt in his mind—for later use. And we'll make it a three-day trip, so I can get a good look at what the country's like out there around his—"

He was cut short by a noise out back in the wagonyard.

Velma jumped to her feet and ran to the back window, peering through the curtains. Clayburn came over beside her. Two of Wheelock's men—Yarborough and a stocky kid wearing two holstered guns—had broken open the fence gate and wandered into the wagonyard.

"It figured," Clayburn said quietly. "Wheelock got tired of waiting and decided it was time to give us another warning. That kid any good with those two guns of his?"

"Sims? *Very* good." Velma watched the two men stroll over between the two stagecoaches. The hulking Yarborough opened the door of the new stagecoach, glanced inside, and said something to Sims. Sims laughed and leaned against the old stagecoach, watching the rear of the house.

Velma looked sharply to Clayburn. "Are we just going to stay in here and let them—"

"No." There was a weird glow in the depths of Clayburn's green eyes. He was almost smiling. It wasn't a nice smile to look at. "Open the door and talk to them."

Her eyes widened with surprise. *"Me?"*

"Uh-huh. You said the kid's good with those guns. But he won't shoot a woman. Don't go out there. Just stand in the doorway." Clayburn put a hand against Velma's shoulder and pushed her toward it. He began backing away from the window.

Uncertainly, Velma moved to the kitchen door. With her hand on the knob, she paused and looked back. Clayburn was gone from the kitchen. Drawing a deep breath, she opened the door and took a single step through it.

Yarborough had climbed up inside the new stagecoach. Sims stiffened a little as she appeared, then relaxed when he saw that her hands were empty and there was no one else behind her. He grinned at her and drawled, "Howdy, Mrs. Lang. Nice evening."

Yarborough looked out from the door of the new stagecoach. The small, deep-set eyes in his brutal face studied her for a moment greedily. Then he glanced over at Sims. "She sure is a good-lookin' one, ain't she."

"What're you two doing here?" Velma demanded, trying hard to keep her voice from trembling.

"Just having a look at your new stagecoach," Sims told her, still grinning. "Somebody sure made a mess of it."

"Sure did," Yarborough's heavy voice chimed in. "Like the way these nice leather seats in here are all shot up." He ducked back inside. There was a tearing sound. When he climbed down out of the coach, there was a long strip of seat leather dangling from his hand.

Velma, shaking with rage, took another step toward them before she could stop herself. "Get out of here! Get out *now*, or I'll—"

"Or you'll *what?*" Sims asked eagerly. "Beat us up? I ain't supposed to hurt you, but I'd sure enjoy *holding* you—just to keep you from hurting yourself, of course."

"What the hell you gettin' all upset about?" Yarborough growled at her, smiling unpleasantly. "This stage of yours wasn't much to begin with."

"Yeah," Sims agreed, without taking his eyes off Velma. "Real flimsy construction. Show her, Yarborough."

"Take this door for example," Yarborough said, gesturing

at the one he'd opened. "I'll bet you I can rip it right off its hinges with no trouble at all." And with that he reached up and grabbed hold of the door with both hands.

He stopped as a quiet voice sounded behind him.

The voice said: "I don't think you'd better do that."

Sims spun toward the voice, both hands jerking to the guns holstered on his thighs. His hands froze just as his fingertips touched the gunbutts.

Clayburn was standing inside the broken fence gate, holding a carbine hip-high, his finger across the trigger.

7

CLAYBURN STEPPED INTO the wagonyard, the carbine in his hands pointing at a spot about halfway between Yarborough and Sims. His smile was thin and his eyes were cold. "Drop your gunbelts," he said softly. "Both of you."

Yarborough stood against the new stagecoach, his huge hands hanging straight down at his sides. He looked from Clayburn to Sims.

Sims didn't move. He stood by the other stagecoach with his fingers still touching the grips of his guns, scowling at Clayburn. A second went by, and then he said, "You can't get both of us before we—"

"Yes, I can," Clayburn broke in mockingly, "and you know I can. You first, of course—because he'd be slower."

Sims considered that, and finally shrugged. "What the hell—you won't get out of town alive, anyway."

"That's my problem. Yours is getting out of this yard alive." Clayburn's voice had gone up a notch, getting a brittle, shaky quality to it.

Sims had heard men's voices get like that before—when they wanted very much to kill and were right on the verge of not being able to control the urge any longer. His hands moved quickly then, going to the buckles of his gunbelts. They dropped away from his hips, falling to the dirt at his feet with the holstered guns.

Yarborough followed his example, unbuckling his gunbelt and dropping it.

Clayburn strolled over between the two men, but closer to Sims. Velma remained rooted where she was, staring at the expression on his face. It was what she had seen in it the previous night when he'd begun drinking himself unconscious after seeing what Yarborough had done to Ryan in the dry-goods store.

The tip of Sim's tongue crept out to touch at the corners of his mouth. "Maybe you don't know what you're getting yourself into, mister. Let me warn you what happens to anybody in this town that—"

He didn't get a chance to finish it. Clayburn took a long sidestep towards him and swung the carbine, one-handed, like a club, slamming the barrel with all his strength across Sims' stomach.

The terrible force of it bent Sims double over the carbine barrel as though he'd been broken in half. A sick moan came out of his wide-open mouth as he fell forward, hitting the ground with the side of his head. He was unconscious before he sprawled over on his back.

The squat, hulking Yarborough moved with surprising speed. He was down on one knee, his right hand yanking the gun out of his dropped holster, by the time Clayburn twisted toward him with the carbine, his finger once more across the trigger.

They looked at each other for a split-second. Then Yarborough dropped the gun and heaved himself to his feet.

"Kick it across the yard," Clayburn ordered. His voice had a wildness in it, and his face was contorted with naked savagery.

Yarborough kicked his gun away from him.

Clayburn went on looking at him with eyes gone dull and lifeless as stone, remembering the way Yarborough had left Ryan the night before. There was no sensible reason for what he was going to do. No reason, except that what he'd been keeping bottled up inside him all this time wouldn't stay bottled up any more—and this was as good a way as any to let it have the explosive release it demanded.

He threw the carbine to Velma without looking at her. "Keep out of this whatever happens," he snarled, and launched himself at Yarborough.

Yarborough sidestepped his rush with startling ease for a man of his bulk, parrying Clayburn's punch with his left hand and slamming his huge right fist across Clayburn's mouth. The blow twisted him around and threw him against the side of the stagecoach. Yarborough's left fist thudded against his side with rib-bending force, spinning him back into a sledgehammer blow that caught him square in the middle of the forehead.

Clayburn hit the ground with the backs of his shoulders, his brain reeling. He rolled away instantly, instinctively, getting his feet under him. Yarborough just stood there waiting, hunched forward slightly with his fists up, a confident smile on his brutal, battered face.

Clayburn squinted up at him through thin-slitted eyes, knowing now what he was dealing with. This Yarborough was a trained boxer.

Wiping the back of his hand across his mouth, Clayburn looked at the blood on it. Then he came up off the ground like an uncoiling spring, swinging a fist in a roundhouse punch at Yarborough's grinning face.

Yarborough sidestepped again, bringing up an arm to parry the punch. But Clayburn's fist stopped in midswing, and he twisted in the same direction that Yarborough had side-stepped. His foot shot out, jamming the boot heel sharply into Yarborough's right ankle. Yarborough howled with pain, automatically jerking his right leg up and grabbing at his hurt ankle.

Then Clayburn hit him, while he was standing on one foot. His bunched right fist slammed against the point of Yarborough's chin, knocking him backward off balance. Yarborough fell on his back. Before he could move again Clayburn landed on his stomach with both knees, driving all the breath out of him. Yarborough was trying to drag air back into his lungs when both of Clayburn's fists, locked together, bludgeoned down across the bridge of his nose, smashing the bone. Clayburn hit him once more, in exactly the same place, before Yarborough's fist pounded into his temple, knocking him sidewise to the ground.

They scrambled to their feet at the same time, facing each other. Clayburn drove himself bodily at Yarborough, forcing him backward toward the stagecoach. He took a sickening blow in the pit of his stomach and a brain-numbing head punch to get it done. But he finally managed to get Yarborough pinned against the coach where his boxing skill would be hampered. He lowered his head as though to butt him in the stomach. Yarborough's knee jerked up at his face. Before the knee could reach him, Clayburn straightened up abruptly, ramming the top of his head into the underside of Yarborough's jaw.

Yarborough's head went up and back. And before he could recover, Clayburn's forearm lashed him viciously across the throat. Yarborough gagged and brought both arms up to fend off another throat blow. Clayburn spread his feet apart and drove a left and right deep into Yarborough's middle. Yarborough sagged forward, his arms dropping, and Clayburn very precisely and deliberately smashed a fist against his broken, blood-dripping nose.

Yarborough fell against him, locking his arms around him and using his greater weight to drag them both to the ground. They landed on their sides, Yarborough grabbing a handful of Clayburn's hair and slamming his other fist at Clayburn's face. His knuckles skidded off the back of Clayburn's head as Clayburn ducked toward him and sank his teeth into Yarborough's cheek, biting down on it as hard as he could. Yarborough screamed and tried to claw him away with both hands, all his science forgotten. Clayburn lowered his right fist and hit him in the groin.

With a sick groan, Yarborough rolled away from him desperately. Clayburn lurched to his feet, panting and swaying as he watched Yarborough drag himself up off the ground. He waited until Yarborough was halfway up, and then he launched a kick at his stomach. Yarborough dropped both hands to catch Clayburn's ankle. But the ankle didn't reach the waiting hands. Clayburn stopped the kick and clubbed both fists across the back of Yarborough's neck.

It bent Yarborough, but he didn't go all the way down. He took it, and then came up, staggering to his feet, slugging at Clayburn with all he had left. But he was dazed and drained now, his punches slow and wild. The rest of it wasn't a fight. It was cold, swift, remorseless demolition.

Clayburn stepped inside the wildly swinging arms and hammered his fist twice into Yarborough's mouth. Yarborough stumbled back, spitting out broken teeth. Clayburn stalked him, knocked down his guard with his left arm, and struck him squarely between the eyes with a twisting, pile-driving right that sent the shock of the impact clear up into his shoulder. Yarborough's eyes glazed over as he stumbled backward again. Clayburn went after him and slammed two long, measured blows into his midsection just below the breastbone, his knuckles breaking through the barrier of thick muscle there and sinking in deep.

Yarborough folded forward, half-turning as his knees bent under him. Clayburn went up on his toes and clubbed his fist down against the hinge of Yarborough's jaw, pounding him face down into the dirt.

But Wheelock's bully-boy wasn't quite finished yet. He managed to drag himself up on his hands and knees, and began crawling toward the place where his gun lay.

Clayburn took a long stride and kicked him in the head.

Yarborough toppled over on his side and stayed that way, his eyes partly open but not seeing anything.

Clayburn dragged air through his open mouth, looking from Yarborough's unconscious hulk to where Sims still lay sprawled on his back. Then he looked toward Velma.

She was standing there holding his carbine and staring at him with stunned eyes, looking dazed and a little frightened. It had dawned on her near the finish that the fight had never hung in the balance; that Yarborough had been doomed to end up this way from the moment Clayburn had started for him.

Clayburn turned away and trudged into the stable, dropping to his knees beside the water trough. He plunged his hands deep in the trough and brought them up, pouring water on his head and face. He did that twice more before he became aware of Velma standing there with a towel in her hand.

She knelt beside him and used a corner of the towel to wipe blood from a cut at the corner of his mouth. He took the towel from her and dipped it into the trough. When it was soaking wet he wrung it out and pressed it against his mouth, his forehead, and the back of his neck. Then he gave her back the towel, grasped the edge of the trough with both hands, and shoved himself to his feet.

Velma rose up facing him. They looked at each other

without speaking for a moment. Then she said, "I asked you what kind of man you were." Her voice was shaky, and her face was too shadowed for him to read its expression. "Well, now I know."

"And you don't like it."

"I didn't say that," she told him, slowly. "No . . . I didn't say that. And now that I know, I guess I don't have to remind you what Wheelock does to people who hurt any of his men."

"No," Clayburn agreed, "you don't have to remind me."

There was a faint catch in Velma's breathing. "And you already knew what you were going to do about it, before you took on those two out there."

"Yes," he told her simply, "as a matter of fact, I did."

Cole Wheelock was in his office over the saloon, eating his evening meal off a tray that had been set on his desk, when Torrey knocked at the door and came in.

"Mrs. Lang's new partner's here," he told Wheelock quietly. "Wants to see you."

Wheelock put down his fork and pushed his chair back a little. Drawing the Colt from his holster, he held it on his thigh, hidden by the desk. Then he nodded at Torrey. "All right. Let him in."

Torrey opened the door wider and gestured. Clayburn stepped into the room past him, coming to a halt in the middle of the office, facing Wheelock behind the desk. Torrey shut the door, drifted to a corner of the room, and leaned against the wall there, his hand hooked on his belt near his gun and his eyes on Clayburn's back.

Wheelock leaned back in his chair, his face blank as his eyes steadied on Clayburn's. "Well?"

"I got into a fight with a couple of your men," Clayburn told him. "They're out in the alley behind this place now, sleeping it off."

Wheelock's eyes narrowed, just a little. "That's too bad," he said softly. "For you."

"They broke into Mrs. Lang's place, started breaking up a stagecoach." Clayburn's voice was unhurried, merely supplying information. "I figured they were drunk. Didn't find out they belonged to you till after I finished with them."

"That's too bad," Wheelock repeated.

"I don't know that it makes any difference to you," Clayburn went on in the same tone, "but I was on my way over here tonight, anyway. To tell you I've persuaded Mrs. Lang we do need to buy protection from you."

Wheelock looked at him without speaking for a moment. Then he said: "On the terms I gave you?"

Clayburn nodded. "On your terms."

A very slight softening occurred around Wheelock's mouth. He raised the gun from his lap and put it down on top of the desk. Then he took his hand from the gun and leaned his elbows on the desk and said, "Yes . . . that does make a difference."

"I was hoping it would," Clayburn said, without any evident humor.

"It does—this one time. We'll say Sims and Yarborough *were* drunk. I'll tell them not to let it happen again." Wheelock paused, and then added: "I'm telling you the same thing."

Clayburn looked faintly surprised. "I figured there'd be no chance of it happening again, now that *you're* insuring us—against accidents."

Wheelock laughed drily. "All right. When you plan to begin making regular runs?"

"We've got to have the new stage patched up first, and repainted. And Mrs. Lang needs a little more operating cash to start off with. She thinks she can borrow it from some rancher named Dixon. Figure on about three days from now."

"Fine. I'll expect to check your books regularly, starting with the very first run."

"Sure." Clayburn's eyes went from the gun on the desk to Wheelock's face. As he turned back to the door, he glanced at the room's single window. It looked across an alley at the rear of a livery stable. Another piece of information—for possible later use.

He had his hand on the doorknob when Wheelock said: "One more thing . . ."

Clayburn looked at him.

Wheelock studied him shrewdly for a few seconds. "I consider this a definite deal. Don't get to thinking about changing your mind, later on. I won't let you."

"Once I decide to do something," Clayburn assured him lazily, "I stick to it." He opened the door and went out.

In the crowded saloon below, Flood had a small corner table all to himself. He was just refilling his beer glass from a second bottle when he saw Clayburn coming down the stairs.

The hand with which Flood was pouring became motionless, and his hooded eyes narrowed. He had spotted Clayburn going up the stairs earlier, though he didn't think he'd been spotted in turn. The clothes Clayburn wore left Flood no doubt about who he was: the man in black, the one he'd narrowly gotten away from behind that canyon.

The man in black was halfway down the stairs when he appeared to notice Flood for the first time. For a fraction of a second their eyes met, and then Clayburn looked quickly away and continued on down the steps.

But Flood had seen the purposeful malice in Clayburn's face during that brief glance. He saw, too, the way Clayburn's hand automatically brushed against the right pocket of his frock coat—and that there was something making a bulge inside that pocket.

Clayburn crossed the saloon without another look in Flood's direction. As soon as he was gone through the door Flood got out of his chair, picked up his rifle, and went out after him into the night.

Clayburn was already half a block away, walking off up the opposite side of the street. Flood stuck to his side of the street as he started to follow. Clayburn didn't pause or look back, but this did not lull Flood into any false sense of safety. He kept to the darker shadows along the walls, and his boots made no sound on the boards under them.

Clayburn reached the mouth of an alley and turned into it, the darkness immediately swallowing him up.

Flood came to an abrupt halt, knowing an ambush setup when he saw one. Changing course, he crossed the street and went around behind a feed-and-grain store. When he was out of sight in back of it, he cocked his rifle and shifted it to his left hand. Drawing the big Bowie knife from its belt sheath with his right hand, he moved on silently, circling behind a group of buildings to reach the other end of the alley—so he could come in behind anyone waiting there to ambush him.

When he reached it, he paused again. The rifle in his left hand came up, and his finger slid across the trigger. He balanced the knife in his right hand, ready for the throw. Then without a sound, he stepped around the corner and into the alley.

His eyes were totally adjusted to the dark by then, and the first thing he saw was the huddled shape in the middle of the alley, with a rifle barrel projecting from it. Flood's nerves spasmed, and he almost fired before he saw what it was: an empty packing box, with a rifle lying across the top of it, pointing at him.

Clayburn was gone.

Flood had known Apaches to play that kind of practical joke. That wasn't what bothered him so much. What got to him was the fact that the rifle had been left pointing toward the rear of the alley, instead of in the opposite direction, where he would have been most likely to appear.

Sheathing his knife, Flood ran his fingers along the stock of the rifle. Sure enough, there was a bullet imbedded in it. His own rifle, the one he'd lost back of the canyon.

Picking it up, he headed back to Wheelock's headquarters. He went through the saloon and up the steps to his own room, next to Wheelock's. Turning up the lamp, he tossed his new rifle on the bed. Then he studied the one that had been returned to him.

Outside of the slug imbedded in its stock, it still seemed in excellent condition. It was even fully loaded. For a while Flood went on looking at the rifle in his hands, frowning. Then he opened the chamber mechanism, raised the rifle to the lamp, and looked down the barrel—and the "joke" took on an increasingly macabre tinge.

There was a chunk of lead stuck halfway down the barrel. It had been jammed in there so that it could not be gotten out without ruining the inside of the barrel. If Flood had tried to fire the rifle before checking it out, it would have blown up in his face.

8

VELMA WASN'T THE only one waiting in the kitchen behind the stage waiting room when Clayburn got back. Greco was there, too. And so was Jace Harcourt.

When Clayburn came in, Velma instantly got to her feet, looking at him questioningly.

"It's all right," he told her. "I bought us a few days' reprieve." He looked at the deputy. "You putting in with us?"

"I'm in," Harcourt said. His voice was low and he still looked scared, but there was a rising stubborness under his uncertainty.

"I figured he'd better move in here with me," Greco told Clayburn. "So we can keep an eye on things while you're gone."

"You can start patching up the new stagecoach, too," Clayburn said. "It's going out when we get back." He looked at Velma. "Get into your riding things and pack whatever we'll need for camping out in the open two nights."

"We're leaving right now?"

Clayburn nodded. "Wheelock's expecting this stage line to start rolling three days from now. I want to see as much of this country as I can in that time."

"All right," she said obediently, and without any further questions she went quickly out of the room and up the stairs.

Clayburn looked after her with an odd half-smile. He was still smiling when he turned back to Jace Harcourt. " 'Fraid you're in for a rough three days, deputy. Greco's likely to bend your ear some, boasting about his past."

Harcourt was surprised to find himself grinning back. "I know. If even half the things he's already told me about himself are true . . ."

"They're *all* true," Clayburn told him. "Trouble is he likes to talk about 'em too much. In this case, though, you'd better soak it all up. More you know about how things like this have been handled in other places, the better you'll get what we have to do here."

"Make up your mind," Greco grumbled. "First you say I'm too gabby, then you say I'm worth listening to."

"They're both true." There was a faint undertone of affection in Clayburn's voice that was rare between them. Neither one of them was what anyone would have considered sentimental. "You better be ready for a lot of riding by the time I get back, Greco. Wheelock can't be held off much longer than that."

"I'll be ready," Greco stated flatly.

Clayburn went up to their room to change into his trail clothes.

When he rode the sorrel he had bought out of Glory Hole that night, few would have recognized him at a distance. His buckskin shirt and Levi's were equally old, and weathered to almost the same neutral color. His boots and his tan, flat-crowned slouch hat were almost shabby from long years of use in all kinds of weather and terrain. He had the bone-handled Colt holstered on his hip once more, and his carbine was in the scabbard secured to his saddle.

Velma, riding out of town beside him, also had a carbine stuck in her saddle scabbard. When they had left the lights of the buildings behind, Clayburn reached over between them and touched its stock. "You know how to use this?"

"I used to hunt with Lang. I didn't do much missing."

"Uh-huh . . . Ever shoot a man?"

"No." After a silence she asked: "Why? Do you think I'll have to?"

"Maybe."

She turned her head in his direction. "I never met anybody like you." She laughed. It was a soft, jittery sound. "When you're in a fight you're ready to use anything that happens to be close to hand. Even a woman."

"Not if you're not up to it," he said simply.

Her answer was direct and emphatic: "It's my stage line. I got no intention of running it for Wheelock's benefit."

They stayed with the pass going north for a couple miles. As Velma started to turn off it into a trail leading east, Clayburn raised up on his stirrups and took a long look around them at the starlit slopes and rises.

Then he lowered himself back into the saddle and asked her, "Any homesteader a little further north who could be trusted to help us in a pinch? One with a good-size barn."

"There's a farmer named Amos Niles a couple more miles up the pass. I know I can trust him. But if it's gun help you mean, no. He's a Quaker or something."

"It's not his gun we'll need. Just his barn."

"Well, he's got one," Velma said, and let it go at that. Clayburn didn't explain, and she didn't ask him to. She was beginning to get used to him. He'd tell her what he had in mind when he was ready to.

Strangely, she no longer minded this, now that she had decided that he knew what he was doing, and could handle whatever was coming. After two years as a widow, it felt good to have that kind of man around again.

They rode east together, following a rising trail that curved and twisted between steep, thickly-timbered slopes. The moon rose and painted the peaks above them with a pale, ghostly glow. The timber got bigger, and the trail steeper. Finally they reached a rolling crest below which the land dropped away from them sharply into a long dark valley.

Velma drew rein. "This is where Dixon's land starts. What he figures he's got a right to, anyway, seeing he was the first one here. Used to be a couple nesters living right down there below us. But not since Dixon imported Wheelock."

Clayburn breathed deeply of the warm night air, his nostrils flaring. "Smells like water close by."

"There's a little stream off to the left there."

"Then that's where we'll make camp for the rest of the night. We'll start off again just before dawn, spend tomorrow circling Dixon's valley."

"What do we say we're doing if any of his men spot us?"

"They won't," Clayburn said. "All we have to do is keep our eyes open, and be careful about where we leave tracks."

She found it natural to accept that about him, too: that he was one of those men who could move through this kind of country in broad daylight without being seen or leaving signs of his passing through it. Kneeing her horse to the left, she led the way down through the trees to a narrow, spring-fed stream. They dismounted and staked out the horses where there was sufficient grass for grazing. Clayburn made the fire by the bank of the stream. He made it small, where the tree trunks would hide the flames and the branches would disperse the smoke. Then he settled back to watch her heat up some salt-beef and coffee.

After they'd finished with the meal, Clayburn kicked dirt over the fire and went to the stream. Squatting on the bank, he cupped water in his hands and washed his face and neck, going easy over the swollen bruise on his forehead and the tender place alongside his mouth.

Velma came down to the stream barefoot, her Levi's rolled up to her knees. She waded into the stream and scooped the cooling water over her face and arms. Then she looked at him and asked, "You still hurting from that fight?" Her voice sounded hoarse.

"Some." The moon was high now, and he could see her face plainly by its pale light. He could see, too, the way the water had run down over her shirt, molding it to the bold curves of her body.

He drew his knuckles slowly across his mouth, not taking his eyes off her. Then he smiled and turned away from the stream, spreading his ground blanket ten feet from the bank. Sitting down on it, he tugged off his boots and stretched out, resting on one elbow and watching her come up out of the stream.

She stopped a few feet from him, looking down at herself. "My shirt's all wet."

"Hang it up to dry."

Her eyes went to him. She could see the reflection of moonlight glinting against the surfaces of his eyes. After a moment her hands reached up and she unbuttoned the shirt and took it off, hanging it from a branch.

He continued to look at her for some time, not saying anything, not reaching out to touch her. Yet she could feel the strength of his will and his desire reaching out from him and seizing her, drawing her toward him like an irresistible physical force. Liquid warmth was flooding through her and her legs were going weak under her. Then she was on her knees beside him, unfastening her hair. It flowed down over her shoulders, and strands of it touched his face when she leaned down to look into his eyes.

"I could waste time being coy about it," she whispered thickly. "I could play at being—"

"Be quiet," he said, and his hands were on her shoulders. His lean, powerful fingers slid up her throat to her cheeks. He gripped her face and pulled her mouth down to his and kissed her savagely, hungrily. She came to him, then, with two years of passion letting go inside her.

It was late on the third morning after leaving Glory Hole when they finally rode down to Dixon's ranchhouse in the far end of the long, grassy valley. By then Clayburn had seen enough of the surrounding country to know how he was going to operate through it when the time came. He had also had a long-distance look, through his army-issue field glasses, at the small spread Wheelock had recently started, between this valley and the town. For his cattle, Wheelock had adopted a brand in the shape of a four-spoked wheel. Which was interesting, considering the -D brand on all the Dixon cattle Clayburn had seen.

Dixon's house was a rambling, well-built one-storey structure, with the barn, bunkhouse, blacksmith shed and other outbuildings fanning out behind it toward a large corral. As Clayburn and Velma dismounted in front of the house, hitching their horses to the rail, Dixon came hobbling out onto the porch on crutches, greeting Velma with genuine pleasure. He was a hard, stubborn-looking man in his late fifties, and it was obvious he had been an unusually strong man. The strength was still there in his face, and in his handshake, when Velma introduced Clayburn as a friend who'd invested in her stage line. But his face was also drawn with permanent pain, and his right leg dangled uselessly, making it impossible for him to move around without the aid of the crutches.

Dixon invited them inside for some refreshingly cold lemonade before sharing a noon meal together. They were joined in the big living room by a rangy, tough-faced man named Rowse, who had been Dixon's foreman for the past ten years. Clayburn noticed the serious attention Rowse paid to what Velma was saying when she told Dixon about what had happened to her new stagecoach.

But Dixon got an uncomfortable, withdrawn look as he heard her story. "You don't know for *sure* Flood and Wheelock had anything to do with that," he pointed out, not quite managing to meet her eyes.

"I do know!" Velma retorted. "And so do you, Dix. You just don't want to think about it, because you know you don't have any control over *whatever* Wheelock does anymore."

Dixon shook his head stubbornly. "The only thing I know about him for sure is this: he's done exactly what I've been paying him to. And he's still doing just that. Whatever else he does is none of my affair."

"Including murdering a man who was only trying to protect his wife?" Velma told him about the lynching of the storekeeper.

Dixon's face darkened, but kept its withdrawn look. "I don't like something like that any more'n you do, Velma. But they brought this on themselves, when they started shielding rustlers and stealing my land. What happens between folks around Glory Hole and Wheelock is *their* problem, not mine."

"It's likely to *become* your problem before long," Clayburn put in quietly. "When you bring a crew like Wheelock's in, you start something that's hard to stop. He's got just about everybody else under his heel now. Makes him feel big, and being the kind of man he is, he'll want to feel even bigger. You'll be the only one left for him to get bigger on. It's like you got a knife in your hand that you can't control. He's gonna turn on you, Mr. Dixon."

"No, he won't. He knows which side his bread is buttered on."

Clayburn's laugh was harsh and mocking. "You won't be able to be sure it's him when it starts. All you'll know is, some of your cattle'll start being missing again. Wheelock'll make a big show of hunting rustlers, maybe even accuse some homesteaders. But you'll go right on missing more cattle all the time."

"He's too smart to try anything like that on me," Dixon snapped.

But his foreman, Rowse, looked troubled as his eyes went from Clayburn to Dixon. "I don't know, boss . . . Tell you the truth, I started getting worried about something like that the day Wheelock picked a four-spoke wheel for his brand."

Dixon gestured impatiently. "He picked it because of his name."

"Sure . . . ," Rowse said slowly, ". . . but it's awful easy to change a bar-D into a four spoke wheel. Too easy."

"If he tries anything like that, I'll deal with him," Dixon said coldly, "when it happens."

"Wheelock's gotten too big for you to take on by yourself," Clayburn told him. "You've probably got a good crew—but they're cowhands, not gunmen. You'd have to join together with the homesteaders and townspeople to handle Wheelock at this point. And you'd best do it now—before he's expecting it."

Dixon glared at him. "And with Wheelock gone, what would happen? I'd be right back where I started—people moving back onto my land, stealing my cattle . . ."

"You'd have no trouble getting in the sheriff with some deputies to deal with that kind of petty cattle stealing."

"Oh, sure. The sheriff could arrest men. But they'd have to be tried in town, and no jury there'd convict." Dixon hammered a fist against his useless leg. "I found that out—the hard way."

Clayburn shrugged. "You and your neighbors are gonna have to learn how to get along together sooner or later. You'll probably wind up with a compromise, letting go of some of the land, in exchange for an end to the rustling."

"No!" Dixon said it with absolute finality.

Velma sighed and changed the subject, telling Dixon about needing to borrow a small amount of cash. "With two of my team horses dead, I've got to buy two more. And I don't have enough on hand. I should be able to pay you back pretty fast, once I have both stagecoaches running regular."

Dixon accepted the change of subject eagerly. "Sure, Velma. I'll give you a note to the bank. They'll let you have the money."

And with that settled, they went into the dining room to eat.

When they rode away after the meal, Velma turned in her saddle and looked back at the ranchhouse, and then looked at Clayburn. "All that talk didn't do much good," she said. "Dix didn't even hear us."

"He heard what we said," Clayburn told her, and there was a malicious glitter in his eyes. "And he'll remember, when something happens that brings it to mind."

It was shortly before dusk when they reached Glory Hole. An hour later Velma's new stagecoach, patched and repainted by Greco and Harcourt, rumbled out of the wagonyard drawn by four strapping team horses. Clayburn was up on the box, handling the reins, with Greco beside him as a guard. As he turned into Front Street, Wheelock came out of his building, followed by Torrey and Flood.

Clayburn reined the teams to a stop in front of them. "Figured we'd go north, the first trip," he told Wheelock politely. "Should be plenty of men up in those mining camps wanting to come back down through here to the railroad."

"Good idea," Wheelock agreed. "You'll probably pick up all the passengers you can handle. Figure three days for the round trip?"

Clayburn appeared a little dubious. "Maybe a little longer. But we should be back this way inside four days, at the most."

Wheelock nodded. "All right. See you then."

"Sure you will," Clayburn said, and looked at Flood. Meeting Flood's hooded stare, he nodded and smiled. It seemed an innocent enough smile.

Wheelock watched him flick the reins and get the empty stagecoach rolling on its way out of Glory Hole. Then he turned with a satisfied smile and went back inside his saloon, followed by Torrey and Flood.

Clayburn kept the stagecoach going north until they were some four miles out of town. Then he stopped and looked back. After ten full minutes, when he was certain they were not being followed, he drove the stagecoach the rest of the way to the farm owned by Amos Niles.

Velma and Clayburn had stopped here on their ride back

from Dixon's ranch to talk to the Quaker farmer. As Velma had predicted, Niles had proved willing to give any help they needed, short of fighting. He came out of his house now to help get the stagecoach and horses hidden inside his barn. Then he went back to the house, leaving Greco and Clayburn to settle down for a wait.

There were still three hours to go before midnight when Velma and Deputy Harcourt rode in, leading a pair of saddled horses. As Clayburn and Greco mounted up, Velma looked at Harcourt's troubled face and snapped: "For God's sake, Jace—will you stop looking so damn worried. They know what they're doing."

"They do," Harcourt acknowledged, "but I'm not sure I do. I know I'm not wearing the badge right now, but I am supposed to be law officer. And this thing we're going to do sure *ain't* legal."

Greco shrugged. "Hell, boy—it's the only way we can cut down the odds. There's just too many Wheelock guns for us to take 'em all on at the same time. So first we gotta sucker some of them guns out of town. Divide and conquer, like Colonel Remsberg used to say."

"You can stop persuading me," Harcourt grumbled. "I said I'd go along with it. But that don't mean I have to *enjoy* it."

Greco laughed. "Cheer up, son. When this is over they'll be making you the new marshal."

Harcourt tried a not too successful grin. "If I'm still alive by then."

"There is that," Greco conceded.

Velma kneed her horse over beside Clayburn's and put her hand on his arm. She looked into his eyes without speaking, the grip of her hand tightening.

He reached out a finger and drew it down the line of her jaw. "Keep your eyes open in town."

"Yes," she said softly, and drew her hand away from him. "Good hunting."

She backed her horse out of the way and watched the three of them ride out into the night.

9

CLAYBURN STOOD MOTIONLESS in the darkness just below the crest of the hill, holding the carbine ready. He had been standing there for quite some time, his head just high enough above the crest, keeping his eyes on the small log cabin down near the bottom of the other side of the hill. From as near as ten yards away no one could have seen Clayburn standing there. He was part of the black night shadow of the fir tree beside him.

The cabin below had a single door and window, and it was these which Clayburn watched. It was a line shack, deep in the mountains to the north of Dixon's long valley. A place for a pair of line riders to put up for the night, while they spent their days combing the innumerable little canyons and wooded slopes, keeping check on Dixon cattle scattered through this part of the mountains for graze.

Clayburn had had a look through his field glasses at this cabin, and the two line riders operating out of it, when he'd circled the area with Velma. There was another line cabin like it far away to the east of Dixon's valley. But that one was for later. This one was the first order of business tonight.

Turning his head in the opposite direction, Clayburn glanced back down the slope on which he stood. In a pocket at the bottom there was a fire, just big enough to heat a branding iron in. By its flickering, reddish glow, he could make out the bent figure of Greco, drawing a running iron out of the red-hot embers. As Greco turned toward where Harcourt was holding down a roped steer, Clayburn returned his attention to the line cabin down at the bottom of the far slope.

Behind him, the steer made a loud bawling sound as the

hot running iron seared its hide. Loud enough to carry quite a distance. The pair of line riders inside the shack must be sleeping mighty sound. This was the third steer to have let out a bleat like that. Clayburn decided Dixon's regular crew were getting careless because they'd gotten too used to having the protection of Wheelock's gunhawks.

He had barely finished this thought when the cabin door suddenly opened and a shadowy figure started to step out into the moonlight.

Clayburn whipped up the carbine and fired, aiming high. The slug thudded into the top of the door, just above the line rider's head. The man jumped back inside, slamming the door shut. Instantly, Clayburn switched his aim and fired again. The second slug tore into the top log framing the single window. Then he shifted over to the other side of the tree, leaning against its trunk, not taking his eyes from the cabin's door and window.

He didn't expect any return fire from the cabin—not unless the two men inside were stupid. They couldn't see anything to aim at, out there in the night. If they had any sense they'd be flat down on the floor by now, with guns in their hands, waiting for further developments and ready to fire if anybody tried to get in.

Which nobody was going to do. Eventually, after there'd been no firing for a long time, the line riders would try opening the door again. When no shots were fired at them, they would head around back of the cabin to their four horses. Line riders had to cover a lot of territory, and needed spare mounts to keep from wearing them out. But the line riders wouldn't find their four horses waiting for them. They'd only find one. Clayburn had slipped down silently and taken the other three away an hour earlier.

That would leave only one man able to ride, and he wasn't likely to go hunting armed rustlers in the dark. The only reasonable thing would be for the rider to hightail it to the Dixon ranch for help.

As Clayburn had expected, no shots came from the cabin. It remained silent and dark. The door had still not reopened when Greco came up the slope and touched Clayburn on the arm.

They went down to the pocket where Harcourt waited, already up in his saddle. The fire had been put out, its ashes mixed with dirt and scattered. The last steer they'd run the iron on had been untied and gone plunging off into the brush after the other two. It would be daylight by the time riders from the Dixon ranch could get back here. Sooner or later, they'd most likely come across one of those steers.

Clayburn and Greco swung up into their saddles and the three of them rode north, each leading one of the horses Clayburn had gotten from behind the line shack.

Greco looked over at Harcourt and asked wryly, "You still worrying about what we're doing not being legal?"

"I've stopped thinking about anything," the deputy said, "except getting through it alive."

Clayburn nodded approvingly. "You're growing up."

He led them along a route over solid rock, where they would leave no trail. The route took them to a stream, and they rode into the middle of it, following its downward course for a while. Then they reined to a halt in midstream and dismounted. Tying prepared canvas sacks on the three "borrowed" horses, they filled these sacks with stones before climbing back into their saddles. When they rode out of the water up the soft dirt of the bank, all six horses were making the kind of tracks that indicated each one was carrying the weight of a rider.

Six mounted and armed rustlers made a formidable group to tackle. It was likely to make the men who would come hunting them go about it cautiously and slowly.

The trail they followed now took them to a small clearing where they'd left the gathering of Dixon cattle they'd combed out of the foothills earlier in the night—some 30 head of them. Bunching them together again, the three men began pushing them farther north, deeper into the mountains, leaving a trail too plain for anyone to fail to find.

They kept the small herd moving along for over an hour, until they entered a large area of forest. With the trees breaking up the herd as they went along, all the three men had to do was to keep pushing them on until all the cattle were gone, wandering off out of sight in a dozen different directions. Even by day, it was going to take the Dixon riders a long time to comb all those cattle out of that forest.

Clayburn led Greco and Harcourt on through the heavy timber, until they reached a rock ravine that they could follow without leaving signs of their going. When they emerged from the ravine they turned south and east.

The other line cabin to the east of Dixon's valley was a long way off. They couldn't expect to reach it until just before dawn. Which exactly suited Clayburn's purpose.

The two men in the line cabin to the east of Dixon's valley came awake with the first light of dawn. They rolled out of their bunks and tugged on their boots without a word to each other. The two of them made an odd pairing. One was a raw kid just turned seventeen. The other was old for a cowhand, and it took him longer to come out of sleep than it used to, so he was never in a mood to talk or be talked to until he had his morning coffee inside him. He began getting the fire going in the stove while the kid went out with the bucket to fetch water.

The kid was back 20 seconds later. He set the bucket down, still empty. "Two of our horses are gone."

The older man glared at him. "What d'ya mean, gone?"

"Just what I said," the kid snapped back at him.

It began to sink in. The two of them hurriedly buckled on their gunbelts and picked up their rifles before going out to saddle their two remaining mounts.

The tracks of the missing pair were easy to follow. So were the bootprints left by the man on foot who'd led them away. After a stretch the bootprints stopped, and from then on their horses were led by a third horse carrying a rider. The tracks led due east, up into a country of high peaks towering over crosscut canyons and vast mesas.

A couple miles farther on the trail the line riders were following disappeared into a stretch of heavy timber. They couldn't find the tracks again on the other side of the timber, but they came across something else: the hoofprints of over 50 head of cattle heading east.

The older rider reined up and stared bleakly at the trail left by the herd. The kid looked at him uncertainly. "Rustlers?"

"You're goddam right, rustlers. Cattle don't bunch up like this and head for where there's no water or graze, unless somebody's driving 'em. You have a look over to the right there. Let's see can we figure out how *many* somebodies."

The older rider swung over to the left of the wide trail made by the cattle herd, moving along slowly and studying the ground. After a time, the kid called out to him: "Looks like three mounted horses on this side!"

"I make out five more this side," the older rider growled. "That adds up to *eight* riders."

The kid cut across the cattle trail to him, hoping he didn't look as nervous as he felt. "Eight rustlers. That's a helluva lot for just the two of us to go chasin' after, ain't it?"

"Exactly my sentiments. Come on, let's get back to the ranch—fast."

The two of them wheeled their horses and raced west, heading for Dixon's valley.

The canyon cut through the heart of the mesa, making one corkscrew bend after another before it finally got all the way through the mesa and opened out of its eastern wall. With so much twisting and turning, it was midafternoon before Clayburn, Greco, and Harcourt got the small herd a quarter of the way through the canyon. At that point there was a side canyon that cut due south toward the Smoke River.

They turned the cattle into this side canyon after setting loose the five horses they'd taken from the line cabins and sending them in ahead of the herd. Once all the animals were well into the side canyon there was no longer any need to push them along. They kept going on their own, drawn by the scent of fresh water up ahead, at the other end. Once the cattle and riderless horses reached the river, they'd begin scattering back to the west, toward the grass and timber around Dixon's valley.

It would be sunset before any riders from Dixon's ranch could possibly reach this side canyon. And they'd have to wait out the whole night before continuing their hunt. If Clayburn's calculations were correct, the riders who came this way would be a bunch of Wheelock's gunmen. Dixon would have sent most of his own crew north the previous night, when the line rider from the cabin out that way rode in with news of night riders, missing horses, and being fired on. At the same time, Dixon would have sent a man to Glory Hole, to demand that Wheelock send some of his gunmen out to do the job they were being paid for.

The riders from the other line shack, east of the valley, would have reached Dixon's ranch shortly before Wheelock's men got there from town. So this was the way they'd be coming, to hunt for the second band of rustlers. Their hunt would keep them pinned out in this area at least through the coming night and part of the following day. How much longer they stayed out after that depended on how determined they were to find the vanished rustlers.

Clayburn wheeled his horse and started west, back down the main canyon, with Greco and Harcourt following. One thing they didn't have to be careful about now was leaving tracks. Not with the way the canyon floor was trampled and churned up by the passage of more than fifty head of cattle. It was almost dusk when they returned to the west end of the canyon. Clayburn reined up just inside the shadowed canyon mouth, motioning the other two to a halt beside him. Taking up the field glass that hung from his neck by a looped strap, he looked through them at the distances west of the mesa.

He didn't see anything at first. But he went on looking, making sure, turning his head slowly and training the field glasses on every direction from which pursuers might be expected to come.

Greco was watching Clayburn, and when he saw his face go taut he knew what it meant. "Riders?"

"Yeah." Through the field glasses Clayburn watched the rising dust to the west, and the tiny, dark figures of mounted men riding out of that dust, following the trail left by the cattle. They showed experience at this—or good leadership. They didn't come on all bunched together. Instead, they were spread out, with flankers off to either side to insure against an ambush. And there was one man riding point, a good distance ahead of the others.

Deputy Harcourt nudged his mount over beside Clayburn.

"Maybe we can still slip out of here before they're close enough to spot us."

"Uh-uh. There's always a chance *they've* got a pair of field glasses, too." Clayburn lowered his own and looked to his right, at the gigantic slide of rocks and boulders piled against the side of the canyon, just inside its mouth. "We'll have to hide in those rocks and let them ride in past us."

He was swinging down from his saddle as he spoke. Greco and Harcourt did the same as he led his horse up into the massive tangle of rocks. They got the three horses well down out of sight between some boulders and the actual wall of the canyon. Then he crawled up between two of the boulders until he could look over the top of a third one, out into the land beyond the mesa.

Greco climbed up on one side of him and Harcourt on the other as he trained the field glasses on the oncoming riders again. They were nearer now—11 of them. Delicately adjusting the focus, Clayburn scanned them. It was as he'd anticipated—Wheelock gunmen—and the one in the lead, carrying a rifle across his saddle horn, was Flood.

Quickly, Clayburn lowered his glasses and checked to make sure the three of them were in deep enough shadow so they couldn't possibly be spotted—even by Flood. And when he looked through the glasses again, he shielded them with his left hand, to be certain no chance ray of light glinted off their lenses.

He watched Flood signal a halt and reach into his saddlebags. His hand came out with a pair of binoculars. Clayburn instinctively cringed a fraction lower as Flood focused on the canyon mouth. Some time went by before Flood finally lowered the binoculars and started his horse moving forward again. The ten men ranged out in a wide-spaced line behind him instantly followed.

Clayburn unlooped the strap from around his neck and handed the field glasses to Greco. "The one in front's the one who shot you. Don't raise up any higher than you are. That Flood's nobody to take chances with."

Greco peered through the glasses. "Oh, brother," he whispered viciously, "would I enjoy paying him back."

"Some other time," Clayburn said. "And some other

place." He took back the field glasses, but didn't raise them to his eyes. The gunmen were quite close now, almost within rifle range.

Harcourt touched Clayburn's arm and whispered, "Shouldn't we get back down to the horses?"

"Yeah. In a—" Clayburn cut himself short. Flood had stopped coming forward again, just out of rifle range. Once more he raised the binoculars to his eyes and trained them on the canyon entrance, studying the mass of rocks among which the three men were hidden.

Beside Clayburn, Harcourt had himself pressed flat against the boulder. "Can he see us?" he asked tightly.

"No."

"Then what's he—"

"He doesn't have to see us to know this is a place for a trap," Clayburn told him quietly. "He's smelling an ambush setup, and not liking it."

Flood lowered the binoculars and turned his head, saying something to the rider nearest him. The other man kneed his horse forward. The two of them rode off to the right of the canyon mouth together, angling toward the mesa.

As they went out of sight around a shoulder of the mesa's outer wall, Harcourt looked again to Clayburn, his eyes questioning.

"Flood's gonna climb the cliff," Clayburn told him, not liking the taste of the words. "Come over the top of the mesa on foot so he can have a look down inside here from above."

Greco had already turned his head and was squinting upward, toward the tops of the looming canyon walls. "Like you said, Clay—this Flood sure ain't something to fool with. He'll spot us easy from up there. And the way he handles that rifle, we won't last two minutes down here. He won't have to bring in the rest of them boys to help him."

Clayburn slid back down between the boulders to the horses. "We've got to hole up further back," he said as Harcourt and Greco came down after him. Grabbing his horse's reins, he started back through the canyon, keeping close to the inner wall so they wouldn't be spotted by the gunmen outside. He didn't have to tell Greco and Harcourt to do the same. They followed in single file, hugging the base of the cliff.

When they were around the first tight bend inside the canyon, they went up into their saddles and rode the rest of the way to the spot Clayburn had in mind. It was a mile inside the canyon, in the left cliff wall. A massive outthrusting of rock shouldered its way up from the base of the cliff there. Behind the formation was a depression in the cliff base, forming what was almost a cave. Clayburn had noticed it when they came through with the cattle early that afternoon. But now that dusk was casting the entire interior of the canyon in deep shadow, the depression behind the formation was invisible.

Unless Flood stopped to investigate every single rock formation on both sides of the canyon all the way through it, he was not likely to investigate this one. With luck.

Dismounting, they led the horses behind the rock formation, down into the darkness of the depression under the cliff base. They couldn't be seen inside there. But neither could they see out of their hiding place. All they could do was stand there and wait, each of them holding his horse still and listening.

They waited a long time before the sound of horses' hooves reached them. Clayburn's right hand tightened on his horse's mane, his left hand grabbing its nose gently, soothing it to silence. Greco and Harcourt were doing the same. None of them seemed to be breathing.

Out in the canyon, the horses drew nearer. Clayburn concentrated on the sounds of their hooves. Two horses.

They came on, and passed the hiding place, moving a little faster than a walk. The sounds of their going diminished as they went on, deeper into the canyon. And then there was silence again.

The darkness inside the hiding place became deeper as night closed in on the canyon outside it. A minute went by. Another.

Then the sound of horses again—a larger group of them. Clayburn's sense of hearing was keyed fine as the horses approached. The sounds of their hooves became louder. The group was directly opposite the hiding place now. Clayburn sucked his lower lip between his teeth and bit down gently, listening.

The group of horses went on past them. After awhile, they could no longer be heard. A minute went by. Another. There were no further sounds.

Harcourt looked at Clayburn, his face a blur in the darkness. Clayburn shook his head from one side to the other once. He had counted what sounded like seven horses in that second group. That left two more, if he was right.

He was beginning to wonder if he had been wrong . . . when the sound of horses' hooves reached them again. Two horses, following the first two groups. A trickle of sweat slid down Clayburn's cheek. He made no move to wipe it away. He didn't move at all. His respect for Flood's know-how had gone up another notch. Anyone who tried to ambush any one of those three groups of riders would find himself trapped in turn by the other two groups.

After the sounds of the last two horsemen had faded away, Clayburn still remained motionless. He stayed that way for three more minutes. Then he removed one hand from his horse and used his sleeve to wipe the sweat from his face.

"All right," he said, and led his horse out of their hiding place, with Harcourt close behind him and Greco bringing up the rear. The floor of the canyon was deeply shadowed, the moon not being high enough yet for its pale glow to reach down into its depths. Clayburn stood holding his horse and taking a last look around while the other two mounted up.

"Come *on,*" Greco growled softly.

Clayburn nodded and swung up into his saddle. Side by side, the three of them turned their horses and started back toward the mouth of the night-shrouded canyon.

They were almost to the first tight bend when the sharp crack of an exploding rifle cartridge split the night silence high above them.

The searing whiplash of a bullet jolted Clayburn sideways out of the saddle.

10

THE BULLET SLASHED downward at a sharp angle, burning Clayburn's right side and glancing off three ribs before plunging on into the neck of the horse under him, breaking its spine.

He was hanging half out of the saddle when the horse started to topple in the same direction. Kicking loose of the stirrups, he hurled himself farther to the left, turning in midair like a falling cat and hitting the dirt on his hands and knees. The dead horse slammed to the ground beside him, and by then he was past the initial shock of the bullet lash and knew what had happened.

He *had* heard eleven horses go past down the canyon—but one of them had been riderless. Flood had not rejoined his men. With all the twisting and turning of the canyon, and the gunmen taking their time riding through it, Flood had been able to almost keep up with them crossing the top of the mesa on foot, ready to throw in an extra surprise element in case of ambush. That much had been due to Flood's cleverness. And bad luck had put him close enough to hear three riders heading back out of the canyon below him.

Flood's rifle cracked out again from the top of the canyon wall. The slug thudded into the body of the horse as Clayburn snatched his carbine from the saddle boot and rolled away into darker shadow. The horses carrying Harcourt and Greco had leaped forward in terror at the sound of the shots, reaching the canyon bend up ahead before Harcourt could manage to start reining his mount around to go back for Clayburn. But before he could make the turn, Greco reached out and grabbed Harcourt's reins, stopping him. Raking viciously with his spurs, Greco drove his own horse forward, dragging the deputy after him the rest of the way around the bend.

Once the shoulder of the cliff was behind them they were safe, out of sight of the rifleman atop the canyon. Greco pulled up short. Wheeling around, he looked back—waiting, listening to the rifle blast out twice more in rapid succession.

Harcourt looked at him in astonishment. "We just gonna *leave* him there?"

"He's got more chance of slipping through on foot," Greco answered tightly. "Horses make too big a target. We stayed back there to pick him up, and we'd be afoot, too."

The sharp crack of the rifle sounded again around the other side of the bend.

Harcourt automatically looked in the direction of the sound, and then quickly back at Greco. "But suppose he's hurt bad? Too bad to—"

"Shut up!"

Something in the way Greco said it made the deputy do just that. He clenched his teeth together, fighting against the need to do something active about Clayburn—anything, other than just waiting.

They waited. There were no further sounds from the other side of the canyon bend—not from the rifle, and not from Clayburn. Harcourt stared at the floor of the canyon where it made the bend, watching for Clayburn to appear. The silence held. He saw no one appear.

It was the sudden slight turning of Greco's head that alerted Harcourt. He peered in the same direction, and saw that one of the shadows at the base of the cliff was moving. Watching in fascination, he saw the shadow continue to ease toward them, coming the rest of the way around the bend. Finally the shadow rose up and became Clayburn striding over to them, carrying his carbine in his left hand.

"Quick," Greco snapped, and drew his left boot out of the stirrup.

Clayburn hooked his toe in the stirrup without a word and swung up behind Greco, his free arm going around Greco's waist. Immediately, Greco wheeled his horse and began kicking all the speed from it that he could get. But carrying double it couldn't keep up with the other horse.

Harcourt raced on ahead, putting more distance between them with every second.

By the time they were out of the canyon and racing across the open country beyond the mesa, Harcourt was more than 200 yards in the lead. Hearing Greco's horse pull to a halt behind him, he reined to a stop and turned back. Clayburn had slid down off Greco's horse, dropped his carbine to the ground, and was wadding a bandana in his hands.

Greco peered down at him. "How bad?"

"Just took some skin is all." Clayburn pulled his shirt out of his Levi's and stuffed the bandana up inside it, against the wound.

Greco leaned down for a closer look. The rifle bullet had made one neat hole in the shirt going in, and another coming out. The area between the holes was wet. "Looks kinda bloody."

"Surface bleeding. It'll stop." Harcourt had reached them by then. Clayburn looked at him and said, "They'll be riding out of that canyon any minute. Get going. Wait for me with Mrs. Lang."

Harcourt stared at him. "What d'you mean, wait for you? You're going with us."

Clayburn shook his head. "I'd slow you up too much."

The deputy's face set stubbornly. "We're not leaving you be—"

Greco cut him short: "Yes, we are." He reached down and touched Clayburn's shoulder with a forefinger. "Be seeing you, Clay."

"Sure."

Greco wheeled and went racing off in the opposite direction from the mesa.

Clayburn glared at Harcourt. "Move, dammit! I can't hide with you advertising where I am."

Harcourt hesitated a fraction longer. Then he spurred his horse away, following Greco.

Clayburn's teeth were clenched as he bent down to pick up the carbine with his left hand. Pressing the wadded bandana tightly to his bleeding wound with his right arm, he began running, heading off at a right angle from the direction Greco and the deputy had taken.

Although this was open country out here, there were plenty of natural places to hide a man—rocks, ground pockets, stretches of tall grass, clumps of brush. Clayburn headed for none of these. He ran where there was no apparent cover at all, and kept running until he heard the sound of horses coming through the canyon. Turning swiftly toward a slight dip in the ground, he dropped flat. He stayed that way, hugging the carbine to him and pressing himself into the ground, keeping his teeth clenched to still the sound of his hard breathing.

Greco and Harcourt were vanishing into a stretch of timber when their pursuers emerged from the canyon—ten mounted gunmen and a riderless horse. They stopped in the mouth of the canyon, waiting until Flood appeared on top of the mesa above them, carrying his rifle. He climbed down to them quickly. As soon as he was mounted they put spurs to their horses and headed toward the stretch of timber.

With Flood in the lead, they raced on past the place where Clayburn lay watching them. But they didn't go far beyond him. Flood suddenly pulled up and jumped down from his horse. Squatting in the middle of a stretch of bare dirt, he leaned down to study the moonlit tracks left by the horses carrying Greco and Harcourt, testing several of the prints with his fingers.

The other ten gunmen with him had stopped, and were watching him impatiently. One of them snapped, "What the hell're we fooling around here for? With one of them horses carrying double, we can catch up easy."

"They *ain't* carrying double," Flood stated flatly. He finished his inspection of the tracks and straightened up. "The third man dropped off somewhere behind us." He turned and looked back toward the mesa. His head moved slowly as his hooded eyes surveyed the moonlit country between him and the mesa, searching for sign of someone walking or crawling.

When he spoke again, it was half to himself: "Each of them horses is carrying just one rider. We can't trail 'em for long by night, if they use any sense at all. And by dawn they'll be too far away for us to ever catch up."

"If there's a man afoot anywhere around here," one of the mounted men grumbled, "*I* sure can't see him."

"He's around," Flood drawled quietly. "And not too far away."

"He might slip back into the canyon," one of the other gunmen said, "and get—"

"He might *try,*" Flood cut in. Not spotting what he was looking for, he climbed back aboard his horse. "Spread out. Try taking him alive if we can. So he can be made to talk about where to find the rest've them."

The riders came back toward Clayburn and the mesa, fanning out until there was some 200 yards between each rider. The two at one end of the line rode past a patch of ground shadow, one on either side of it, without either of them noticing anything to indicate that a man was part of that shadow.

Clayburn watched them go away from him toward the mesa. His eyes followed them, but the rest of his head didn't move at all. He saw them reach the mesa and congregate at the canyon mouth.

Leaving two mounted men there to block the way into the canyon, Flood and the rest turned and came slowly back in Clayburn's direction, spreading out farther apart this time. Clayburn held himself where he was with an effort as they approached, stretched flat out in the open, not breathing as he made himself part of the ground and the shadow.

One of the riders came close—close enough for Clayburn to have reached out and touched the horse's leg. If the rider had been Flood, that would have been the end of it. But the rider wasn't Flood—and he wasn't looking down. His attention was on patch of tall buffalo grass up ahead; a likely place for a man to try to hide. So he kept going toward it without seeing the prone figure that his horse nearly stepped on.

Moving his eyes, Clayburn watched the gunman ride straight into the patch of buffalo grass, turn, and ride back through it again. The rider kept this up until the entire patch had been trampled flat. Then he rode off to another likely bit of cover.

For almost an hour the riders combed the area, searching behind every rock and scrub pine, trampling bushes and grass, investigating ground pockets and stands of timber. Finally, Flood called a halt and told his men to make camp in front of the canyon. "We'll set out after him come morning, soon's there's light enough for me to find his tracks."

"He could be a far way off by then," one of his men pointed out.

"Not far enough." The only emotion in Flood's voice was a tinge of boredom at having to state the obvious. "He's on foot, remember? We'll ride him down by noon. At the latest."

The rest of his men joined the two at the canyon mouth and started a fire. Flood himself took another swing around the area, stopping now and then to study a stretch of bare earth that couldn't be crossed without leaving tracks. Clayburn, watching him, was relieved to see that Flood *could* make mistakes at this game. Flood was assuming that his men had done an efficient job of combing the area where Clayburn lay, and was confining his last search to areas a good distance farther away from the canyon.

Not finding what he was looking for, he finally joined his men for the night meal. When they were finished eating, and the fire had been smothered, most of the men bedded down for the night. Flood assigned the night lookout stints, climbing to the top of the mesa to take the first watch himself.

All this time Clayburn had remained where he was. And he continued to stay there. The moon was high now, and he had no intention of moving so long as it was Flood up there, keeping an eye on the area.

The waiting was not entirely wasted time. Lying there, not moving, gave his side a chance to stop bleeding. By the time Flood finally climbed down from his lookout post, even the wadded bandana stuck fast to the wound was dry. It was caked with congealed blood, and his whole right side hurt, but not enough to slow him up.

Flood roused one of his men, and settled down to get some sleep himself. Clayburn waited some 15 minutes after the new lookout took over—long enough for the man to get bored with staring out at the empty night. Then he began moving out, snaking his way along the ground. He had worked out his route during the hours of waiting, and he followed it now—a circuitous, erratic route that took advantage of every groundswell and natural stretch of shadow that would cloak his passage.

It was slow going, but it brought him at last to the nearest stand of timber. Clayburn paused, looking back. The man was still up there on the mesa, gazing off in another direction. There was no sign of any activity from the men bedded down outside the canyon. Clayburn worked his way deep in amongst the trees before climbing to his feet. He stood there for a bit, breathing deep and slow, going over one last time the odds against him.

He had one great disadvantage in addition to being on foot. Though he had spent two days with Velma exploring the country before meeting Dixon, it had been a superficial look. You needed weeks, not days, to explore that much territory thoroughly. Much of the country that lay between here and Glory Hole was unknown to him. He had no way of knowing, beforehand, if each route he chose along the way was the best one for his purpose. And in places he would have no way of knowing exactly what he was heading into.

Flood, on the other hand, had had a year to learn every foot of this country. And he had the kind of background that would enable him to make skillful use of this knowledge in hunting Clayburn down. He would know the places where a man could find water and the places where he might hole up. If he found sign of Clayburn entering an area he would be able to figure out ahead of time what Clayburn would run into and where he'd be likely to wind up.

But that was a handicap Clayburn would have to operate under no matter which direction he went in. Since he couldn't predict the pitfalls of the country ahead of him, he was left with no alternative but to deal with them as they came.

So, finally, he decided he would have to stick with his original plan: strike out straight for Dixon's valley, aiming to reach it by the following night, using the darkness then to cut across the open valley to the ranch. If he could manage to get that far without being caught, he'd be safe. He could tell Dixon his horse had broken a leg while he was out riding, and borrow another to carry him the rest of the way.

Going on through the timber until he reached a clearing, Clayburn looked up at the stars and got his bearings. Then he headed west, moving with a long, easy stride that would eat up distance without tiring him. He didn't look back. There was no need to do that. Not yet. Not until the coming of dawn.

Dawn found him deep inside a maze of canyons and ravines east of the valley. In the night he had entered what had started out as a narrow, steep-sloped pass leading directly toward his objective. He had been hiking through it for two hours when the passage suddenly doubled back on itself. It was then that he had climbed to the top of the high slope and discovered he was in the middle of the maze of stone and rock spreading out beyond him as far as he could see in the ghostly moonlight.

Backtracking for two hours, plus more hours spent finding another way through, would have been too risky. So he had picked out a canyon that seemed to cut west toward the valley, and had gone down the far slope and into it.

The canyon did lead west, and once he was deep into it he could not get out anyway, without turning back. The walls on either side of him rose sheer toward the sky, impossible to climb. It was two hours before dawn when he'd heard the trickling of water, and followed the sound to a small spring at the base of a cliff. He had rested there for awhile, drinking deeply from time to time. Not merely slaking his thirst, but also filling his belly to compensate for the food he hadn't eaten—and wouldn't be eating for some time to come. Finally he had gone on, moving at the same steady, ground-consuming pace he had been using all night.

The canyon seemed to continue endlessly, not opening into anything, its wall still rising straight up without a break or a trail out. He was still in the same canyon when the first gray light of dawn began spreading across the night sky above him. He kept going, still with that long, easy stride. But the muscles of his legs were beginning to lose their springy resilience. He was having to push a little now to keep to the same pace.

In the dissolving darkness, he saw something looming ahead of him. His mouth thinned as he kept on toward it, sensing what it was even before the growing dawn light showed it to him: a mile ahead of him the canyon came to a dead end.

Clayburn's stride didn't slacken. To go all the way back through the canyon now would increase tenfold the danger of his running smack into his pursuers. First he intended to make damn sure there was no way out at this end. He was half a mile from the canyon's end when a surge of relief swept through him. The dead end was not a sheer wall. The canyon narrowed there, and was blocked by a massive mound of rocks and boulders, perhaps piled up there by a river which had rushed through this canyon eons ago. It was steep and high, but it could be climbed.

Dawn was becoming morning when he reached the obstruction and began to climb. It was impossible to go straight up. In places the way above him was blocked by overhanging boulders. In others, loose rocks made him seek out another route to avoid the danger of starting a slide and getting himself crushed under it. For every few yards upwards he managed, he had to detour to one side or another for twice that distance; and several times he was forced to climb partway back down and find another route. There was only one compensation: if Flood and his gunmen found his trail and followed it into the canyon, they'd never be able to get their horses over this pile-up.

It took him over an hour to reach the top. By then he was drenched with perspiration and the bullet rip along his right side had opened up a little. It wasn't bleeding much, but his whole side throbbed, from his shoulder clear down into his hip.

What he saw on the other side made it worthwhile. Below him the land dropped away into a small valley locked in by mountain slopes. It was about a quarter-mile across and half a mile long, with plenty of high grass and a scattering of trees. And there were six head of cattle in it, grazing. Which meant there had to be a way from this small valley to the larger one where Dixon had his ranch.

From his position atop the pile-up, Clayburn could see two possible ways out of the little valley. One was off to his left at the end of the valley: the open mouth of another canyon, which seemed to lead south. The other way was directly across from him, where the grass sloped upward into a notch between mountain slopes to the west. Clayburn decided for the notch.

The climb down the pile of rocks and boulders was a little easier than the climb up had been. He reached the valley floor in half the time and headed directly across it through the tall grass. But his legs were going leaden by then, and the accumulated fatigue was getting to his nerves, warning him he would have to find a place to hole up and get a little sleep soon before pushing on much farther.

He found the kind of place he was looking for when he reached the top of the valley's far slope. There the ground leveled off for a space before climbing again into the mountain notch. And on either side of him were heavy stands of timber.

Following a route over bare rock and being careful to leave no sign of his passage, he reached the edge of the timber to his right. There he turned and looked back the way he had come, scanning the little valley, studying the mound of rocks and boulders blocking the canyon through which he'd come, and the open mouth of the other canyon.

Leaning his back against a tree trunk, he got out a cigaret and lit it, sucking the smoke in deep to feed some of the hunger beginning to gnaw at him. While he smoked, he calculated the timing involved—if he counted every one of the chances that could go against him.

Finally, he decided he could allow himself two hours' sleep. No more than that. Finishing the cigaret, he ground it out and buried it carefully under a low-spreading juniper. Then he crawled in among the bushes under the trees, stretched out on a mound of pine needles, and willed himself into immediate sleep.

He woke exactly two hours later. He came awake completely the instant his eyes opened, the way a hunted animal does when its survival instinct is alerted. There was no vestige of sleepiness left in Clayburn as he picked up the carbine and rose to his feet. His legs felt rested and the dulling effect of fatigue was gone. But his right side was sore and stiff as he moved silently through the trees to the edge of the timber.

He stopped behind the last tree at the edge, and then shifted slightly to one side, just enough to see past it, down into the little valley. All was exactly as he had last seen it. The cattle had drifted to different positions, that was all. There was no one in the valley, and no sign of anyone's having passed through it. Clayburn studied the top of the boulder pile and the open mouth of the other canyon. After that, his eyes scanned the little valley again. He took his time about it. Then he studied the area nearer to him, and the slope above him leading up into the mountain notch, taking his time about that, too.

Finally he stepped out from behind the tree, into the open. He stood there, apparently relaxed but poised to jump. Nothing happened. He listened for a time; heard nothing but the twitter of a few birds. Yet the tight-coiled feeling in his middle would not let go all the way.

Frowning slightly, Clayburn finally turned and started up the incline toward the notch between the slopes. The incline grew steadily steeper, until it became so steep that he began to wonder if those cattle *had* gotten into the little valley by coming through this way.

By the time the incline finally leveled off a bit, almost an hour later, he was panting from the steady climbing. Pausing to catch his breath, he turned and looked back the way he'd come. From this height on the mountain shoulder he could see down over the timber in which he'd slept, to the small valley far below. Clayburn stood there, gazing down at it, giving himself a short rest before going on. As his breathing eased, the hunger pangs asserted themselves again, more sharply this time. He stuck another cigaret in the corner of his mouth and lit it, cupping the flame of the match with his hand.

As he shook out the match flame, the tiny joined figures

of a horse and rider appeared out of the open-mouthed canyon below, coming into the little valley. Then two more mounted men rode out of the canyon after him, followed by another pair.

Clayburn took the cigaret from between his lips and made a bitter count of the rest of them as they emerged into the grassy pocket down there, coming on past the cattle. They were all there—all eleven of them.

Flood and his private little army.

11

CLAYBURN BACKED INTO the shadow of a shaggy spruce, keeping his eyes on the figures in the little valley below. He stuck the cigaret back in the corner of his mouth. The fingers of his right hand broke the match in half and stuffed the two pieces down in the hip pocket of his Levi's. He took a deep drag at the cigaret, letting the smoke trickle slowly from his mouth and nostrils, to float up along the trunk of the tree and be dispersed in the overhanging boughs.

Ten of the tiny mounted figures below had drawn to a halt. The other one had dismounted and was investigating some fallen rocks at the bottom of the boulder pile-up. That would be Flood, reading the signs of Clayburn's climb down that pile.

Clayburn had been trailed by other men in the past. He knew beyond a doubt now that none of them had been a match for Flood. Clayburn hadn't left much of a trail for anyone to follow during his long night's hike. But Flood had found what trail he'd left—and been able to figure out his changes in direction closely enough to scout the stretches where he'd left no trail, until he picked up his tracks again. He'd obviously found sign of Clayburn's entrance into the long canyon—and knowing of the barrier at this end, had taken another way to get here through the other canyon. Evidently a shorter way.

Clayburn watched Flood turn from the boulders and start across the grass on foot, leading his horse and studying the ground.

Taking another slow drag of smoke into his lungs, Clayburn continued to watch as he worked out the change in tactics required by the fact that they had trailed him this far. There was no sense in rushing, now, to put more distance between himself and his pursuers. When it came to covering distance over ordinary ground, the horses gave Flood's bunch too much speed for him to cope with.

With them this close, it wasn't distance that he had to put between himself and them. It was obstacles he had to look for now—obstacles that a man on foot could climb but a horse would have to circle around. If he could make them keep losing time that way, it would cut down the advantage of their superior speed. If necessary, he would have to play hide-and-seek with them until dark, when Flood would no longer be able to find his tracks.

But it would be a long time before night came. He had most of the day still ahead of him, and two special dangers that he would have to beware of every minute of that time: he must be careful not to let himself get boxed in someplace where he couldn't get out without walking straight back into their guns; and he mustn't be spotted out in the open where they could ride him down before he could reach some obstacle their horses couldn't climb.

Clayburn took a last drag at the cigaret and dropped it, grinding it out under his heel. He squatted and picked it up, sticking it in his hip pocket with the broken match. There was a faint trace of ash left on the ground. He scattered it with his fingertips, mixing it with the ground dust.

Flood had remounted and was leading the other ten riders across the grass to the slope up which Clayburn had come. It had taken Clayburn almost an hour to reach this height. It would take his pursuers longer. They would have to climb up the steep incline the way he had, on foot. And they would be slowed considerably by having to drag their horses up with them.

Clayburn stood up and turned away, striding into the thick timber to his left. When he was deep inside the forest he began angling upward again. The rise of the mountainside became steadily steeper. The trees through which he moved became smaller, farther apart. He kept climbing, until the ground suddenly leveled—and then came to an abrupt end.

He found himself standing on the top of a cliff that stretched away to either side of him as far as he could see. Below him, the eroded face of the cliff dropped a hundred feet to a timbered flat that twisted its way between two high shoulders of the mountain.

Clayburn squatted at the edge, studying the cliff drop below him. Then he moved off a hundred feet to the left and started climbing down. It wasn't a difficult climb. There were plenty of small projections and holes in the cliff to serve as toeholds all the way down, and he reached the bottom in a matter of minutes. But no horse would be able to come down that way. And as far as he could see in either direction, there was no trail or series of ledges by which horses could be led down that cliff. Which put the first obstacle between him and his pursuers. What he couldn't be sure of was how far Flood's bunch would have to circle to get around the cliff.

Turning away from it, Clayburn hiked west through the timbered flat.

An hour later he reached a small clearing and squinted upward. The sun was directly overhead. Half of the day gone—and he was still alive. But with the second half of the day to go.

The flat ended half a mile farther on, where it came to the juncture of three uprearing shoulders of mountainside. Clayburn climbed the lowest one, the one between him and the west. Reaching the top, he paused to catch his breath and have a look at what lay to the west.

The mountain sloped down from him to the wide sweep of a grass flat before rising up again to sharp, towering peaks. And just beyond those peaks, if Clayburn was judging his position correctly, lay Dixon's valley.

Clayburn turned and studied his back trail. To the east he could see the long gash marking the cliff down which he'd climbed. It didn't look like much of a cliff from this distance. Carefully, he surveyed all the country between it and where he stood—the timbered flat, the forested slopes, and bare rock ridges. It was the kind of country men could travel through without being seen, unless you took the time for a detailed inspection of it.

He took the time. He studied the country one section at a time, giving extra attention to the most likely approaches. He was studying a section of the forest a mile below down his back trail when he saw dust rising up out of the branches of the trees.

Clayburn froze, watching it. The dust continued to rise, moving slowly in his direction. He couldn't see anything else through the heavy foliage down there. But there was no question about what it was he was looking at. Only a group of horses could be stirring up that much dust.

Clayburn turned quickly in the opposite direction, to head down across the grass flat to the west.

He stopped himself abruptly.

There were five mounted men riding into the grass flat out of the timber to the north, spreading out a couple hundred yards apart as they came on towards the position where Clayburn stood.

Flood had split his men into two separate hunting parties, and Clayburn was caught between them.

Clayburn twisted to the right and went back down off the crest. Getting into a heavy stretch of pine forest, he cut through it toward a higher shoulder of mountainside, to the south. He reached it and climbed swiftly, using all the power of his long legs to drive himself upward. He had to find another obstacle that he could put between himself and the horses of his pursuers. If he didn't find what he needed in this direction, soon, he'd have to double back. Try to slip unseen between the two groups of gunmen and search in the opposite direction.

If Flood hadn't been among his pursuers, Clayburn's tactics at this point would have been much different. In a forest like this one there were plenty of places where he could hole up and not be found—by most men. But that didn't apply where Flood was involved. If Clayburn stopped moving now Flood would find him, sooner or later.

His legs were shaky with weariness by the time he reached the crest of the mountain shoulder. His right side ached and his breath whistled in and out of his clenched teeth. But what he saw ahead of him made the climb worth it. The ground swept downward from the crest, and then rose again sharply as it came up against the bare rock wall of a long, high ridge. The ridge formed a barrier a horse couldn't possibly climb. But it looked as if a man could.

Clayburn hurried down the slope to make sure. Ten minutes later he was at the base of the looming wall of rock. That close up the wall turned out not to be the sheer rise it had seemed from a distance, but it was still something a horse couldn't manage. Erosion had cut deep horizontal and vertical fissures in the ridge, and towering stone pillars clung to it like gigantic tree trunks leaning against the wall and reaching almost to its saw-toothed crest.

Pausing only long enough to work out his route, Clayburn began his climb. Halfway up he found himself stuck in a place where the only way to go on was by way of a narrow rising ledge. The ledge was less than five inches wide in places, and covered over with a deep accumulation of loose rock rubble. Clayburn weighed the danger of slipping off that ledge against the danger of wasting time going back down to find a safer way up. He glanced across at the mountain shoulder over which he'd come. His pursuers were not yet in sight, but they might appear any minute. If they showed up while he was still climbing, he'd be a helplessly exposed target for their rifle fire.

He decided for the ledge, and started up it immediately. It was slow, risky going, one carefully placed step at a time. The loose rock rubble shifted under his weight with each step. Pebbles began trickling off the ledge and rolling down the ridge below him. But he made it almost to the top before what he'd been most afraid of happened.

A whole section of rock rubble suddenly slid out from under him. He braced his legs to hold himself in place, leaning against the side of the wall and hooking his fingers into a crack and clinging to it with all the strength of his hand. He didn't go over. But a mass of the rock rubble did, spilling over the lip of the ledge and sliding all the way down the ridge with a crashing noise that echoed and re-echoed through the mountain slopes.

Clayburn cursed silently. With the noise of that rock slide to guide them, every one of his pursuers would be closing in on this spot as fast as they could come.

He worked his way up the rest of the ledge, and then paused to look back. Flood's riders were still not in sight. Making it the rest of the way to the top took him a matter of minutes. Standing on the spine of the ridge, he saw that the ridge extended for a couple miles in either direction. On the other side of it was a multitude of thick-forested mountain humps and slopes—and some miles beyond these, the foothills edging Dixon's valley.

The sound of horses brought Clayburn twisting around. No riders were visible, but from the sound of it they were coming up the other side of the mountain shoulder back there. Clayburn's cheek muscles tightened, tugging the corners of his mouth and flattening the taut flesh across his cheekbones, turning his expression into something sullen and vicious. He slid down the other side of the ridge, stopping when he was just far enough below the spine to be out of sight.

He took off his hat and put it down beside him. Taking the carbine in both hands, he slid a finger across the trigger. Then he raised his head just a little, looking over the spine of the ridge—hoping that one of the riders would be Flood. With Flood dead, he could lose the rest of them in less than an hour.

Four mounted gunmen came riding up into view over the crest he was watching. None of them was Flood. But Clayburn's expression did not change, and he stayed where he was. The four riders came on down the slope with the careless speed of hunters trailing something harmless. They needed a lesson that would slow their hunting in the future. And Clayburn needed something that would make up for having been on the run for an entire night and most of a day without striking back.

He waited until they were inside carbine range. Then he raised up on his knees with the carbine stock cradled to his cheek and shoulder.

The nearest rider saw the movement atop the ridge and let out a warning yell. He was wheeling his horse away when Clayburn got him in his sights. The carbine roared and bucked against his shoulder. The slug ripped downward through the lead rider's hat and hammered into the side of his skull, kicking him out of the saddle and dropping him to the ground in a limp, grotesque sprawl.

The other three gunmen were already racing away as Clayburn levered another shell into the firing chamber and switched aim to the next nearest target. It was a fast-moving target, the rider bent low against the neck of the horse he was spurring away. Clayburn got off a snap shot at him just before the target got out of range. The horse went down head first, sending its rider somersaulting through the air in a high arc. The man slammed to the dirt on his face and chest, and dragged himself behind a rock. Clayburn levered the carbine and looked for the other two riders. They were out of range, racing away back over the rise.

Clayburn's lips thinned back in a wolfish smile. He slid down below the spine and put on his hat. Getting to his feet, he climbed the rest of the way down the ridge. The sudden release of violence had cleared his thinking. As he headed into the forest below he decided it was time for another change in tactics. He was tired of walking. He wanted a horse.

If Flood held to his methods, he would be splitting his men into two groups again—one group heading in one direction around the ridge, the other circling it the other way. It was up to Clayburn to find the means to split one of these groups into still smaller units.

He was climbing through tall stands of pine when he heard the sound of running water. Cutting over towards it, he came to a narrow stream rushing down the mountain side. Without pausing, he waded into the water. Keeping to the middle of the stream, he started to follow its downward course.

There were stones imbedded in the stream's bottom mud. Clayburn's boots kicked several of these over as he waded down through the rushing water. He came to a place where slim branches of willows on either bank formed a dropping green bridge across the narrow stream. Holding the carbine in front of his face, he shoved through. Then he stopped and turned around. His passage had torn leaves from the slim branches, and a couple of twigs dangled, broken.

Clayburn crouched and went back under the willow branches, without touching them this time. He started back upstream, careful now to kick over none of the stones in the bottom.

A tracker of Flood's experience would not miss the signs that meant the man he was after had gone downstream. But Flood was too clever to ignore the possibility that these signs had been left behind deliberately, to mislead him while his prey actually doubled back upstream. So Flood would split whatever men he had with him into two groups; one group heading downstream and the other hunting upstream. To search for sign of his leaving the stream at any point, each of these groups would have to split in half—one half riding up one bank, the other up the other bank. Whether Clayburn could make use of this or not depended on the size of each unit.

He went past the place where he had originally entered the stream, and continued to wade upward. The incline grew steadily steeper, and the force of the rushing water against which he had to push himself didn't make it any easier. But about a mile farther up he found the sort of thing he was looking for: dense bushes of creeping juniper lined the banks of the stream here.

Clayburn waded to his right, until he was standing in water that was only up to his ankles. Bending at the knees, he jumped for the bank—landing in the middle of a clump of low juniper. There was no sign of his having left the stream at that point, unless someone like Flood came this way, someone smart enough to beat aside the bushes along the bank, for a look underneath them.

Picking his route where he would leave as little sign as possible, Clayburn moved away from the stream, and then began circling back down the slope. He moved silently through the shadowed forest, his hearing acutely attuned every step of the way. And he came to an instant halt, going down in a crouch, when he heard the sound of a horse moving between him and the stream.

He remained crouched, listening, until he was sure of what he heard: a single horse. Soundlessly, Clayburn drifted toward the sound through the bushes. When he was close enough, he went down on his knees, peering out through the thick foliage. The horse he had heard was a strapping gray, moving at a slow walk. The man riding it wasn't Flood. It was a short, wide-set man, holding the reins with one hand and a Colt held ready in the other. There was no one else in sight.

Clayburn drifted backward until he could no longer see the horse and rider. Rising to his feet, he hurried back up the slope, cutting over until he reached the screen of juniper along the stream bank. There he turned his back to the stream. In front of him was a stretch of soft dirt, between the juniper bushes and a stand of young fir trees. Deliberately, Clayburn walked across the dirt, his bootheels sinking in deep.

When he got to the other side of the dirt area, he turned and circled back around it to the stream. Getting down, he slithered out of sight under the growth of junipers. He put the carbine on the ground, reached into his left sleeve, and drew the knife from the sheath strapped to the inside of his forearm. Holding it ready, the blade protruding upward as an extension of his clenched fist, he waited.

The sound of an approaching horse was not long in coming. Clayburn held his breath, listening tensely. It had to be accomplished with no noise that would carry to the others, or he was in worse trouble than before. The horse came very near, and halted. Clayburn could see nothing through the bushes that concealed him. He had to depend, now, entirely on his sense of hearing.

There was a creak of saddle leather. Clayburn remained as motionless as stone, listening to the small sounds that followed. Then he reached with his left hand and parted a juniper bough slightly.

The gunman squatted beside his horse with his back to Clayburn, studying the boot tracks in the stretch of dirt. After a moment, he started to rise.

Clayburn came to his feet at the same time and reached him with two long, soundless strides. His left hand whipped around the man's throat, chopping edgewise across his Adam's apple with a terrible force that choked off his outcry before it could reach his open mouth. At exactly the same time, Clayburn slashed the knife blade down across the knuckles of the man's right fist, causing his fingers to spring open and lose the gun before he could squeeze its trigger.

The gunman sagged forward, both hands clutching upward at his agonized throat, a small gagging sound issuing from his contorted mouth. Clayburn dropped the knife and drew his own gun, clubbing him brutally across the side of the head.

The man's legs buckled under him and he sank to the ground as Clayburn grabbed the reins of the shying horse. Clayburn slipped his gun back in its holster, picked up the knife, and slid it back into its hidden sheath inside his left sleeve.

He led the horse to the screen of junipers and got his carbine. Then he led the horse away, waiting until he was far beyond earshot of the stream before he swung up into the saddle and rode on.

12

HAVING A HORSE UNDER him changed everything. Clayburn was out in Dixon's valley in less than an hour, keeping well out of sight of the ranch-house as he cut straight across towards the pass above Glory Hole.

He knew Flood would find his trail again, as he had each time before. But this time it wouldn't be the same. Finding the few signs Clayburn left behind him would be slow work, even for a tracker like Flood. Before, Flood and his riders had always been able to make up the time because the man they were after was on foot and couldn't cover much ground fast.

But now Clayburn was riding a horse, too. And it gave him more speed than they had. Their pursuit was slowed by their having to circle and search all along the way. All Clayburn had to do was keep going, as fast as the big gray horse could carry him without playing out, increasing the distance between him and his pursuers with every mile he covered.

It would be at least two hours before Flood managed to trail him as far as the long valley. Another hour after that it would be dark, and Flood's bunch would have to wait out the night before continuing their hunt. By morning even Flood was going to have a hell of a time trying to trail him through a valley that was crisscrossed constantly by other horsemen and hundreds of head of cattle.

It was several hours after nightfall when Clayburn reached Niles' farm four miles above Glory Hole, and turned the gray into the big barn. Three figures hurried to him out of the shadows as he lowered himself wearily and stiffly to the ground beside the stagecoach. Velma Lang reached him first, coming at him like she intended to throw herself into his arms. But when she was facing him she stopped herself and just stood there, looking at him.

Harcourt shook his head disbelievingly. "You made it."

"I kept telling you that," Greco said in a bored, long-suffering tone. He eyed Clayburn appraisingly. "How's the side?"

"It hurts." Clayburn looked back to Velma. "What's happened in town?"

It took her a moment to get her voice working. "Just what you already know," she said unsteadily. "One of Dixon's hands rode in and Flood rode out with a bunch of gunnies."

"Nothing else? You haven't heard about any trouble brewing between Dixon and Wheelock?"

"No. Were you expecting any?"

Clayburn nodded. "We changed the brands on some of Dixon's cattle. To Wheelock's brand, making a pretty obvious job of it. I figured Dixon's men would've run across one of those steers by now."

"That's a pretty rotten trick to pull on Dix," Velma said slowly.

"Dixon brought Wheelock into this country," Clayburn told her dispassionately. "He can do his part in getting rid of him. I'm not expecting Dixon to fight Wheelock for us. I just wanted to make sure Dixon wouldn't be inclined to send Wheelock any help, when he needs it."

"Wheelock isn't going to need help, the way things stand. He's still got too many guns left in town for the three of you to go against."

Greco laughed softly. "We know. We're about to do something about that."

Velma didn't look at him. Her eyes were still fixed on Clayburn, and she'd suddenly lost interest in the subject they'd been discussing. "How bad is that wound you got?" she asked quietly. "You look ready to drop."

"I'm just tired. And hungry."

"Oh . . ." She grasped at something she could do for him. "I'll go in the house and fix you a meal."

"Make it a big one. And some clean cloth for a bandage."

As she hurried out of the barn, Clayburn turned to Greco. "I gotta get some sleep. You and Harcourt'll have to handle the next bit without me."

Greco shrugged. "Sure. I could do that one all by myself, if I had to."

Harcourt was looking from Clayburn to Greco uncertainly. "Do *what?*"

"According to Mrs. Lang," Greco told him, "there's never more than a few gunhawks stayin' in the house out on that little spread Wheelock took over. Well, them boys are about to have night-rider trouble."

The deputy frowned at him. "Us?"

"Uh-huh. Us. We're gonna shoot up Wheelock's ranch-house. The boys staying there'll decide they better head for town and tell Wheelock."

A grin spread over Harcourt's face as he got it. "And he'll send a bunch of his guns out there to see what's going on—leaving us less to deal with in town."

"That's the idea, son. You like it?"

"Against Wheelock . . . yeah, I like it."

Greco laughed and clapped him on the shoulder. "Okay, deputy, let's get at it."

They rode out into the night while Clayburn was unsaddling the gray horse in one of the empty stalls. After he'd wiped the horse dry, he saw to its feed and water. Then he tended to himself. Tugging off his boots, he stripped to the skin. He slammed his Levi's and shirt against a stall post until most of the trail dust was beaten out of them. Then he went out to the pump behind the barn.

Filling the bucket, he raised it over his head and dumped the water over himself. He did this several more times, and then knelt under the pump and soaked the bandana stuck to his side until he was able to peel it off the bullet rip without causing much new bleeding. He cleaned the wound carefully, and then washed himself from head to foot. He was rising to his feet when Velma stepped out of the barn and came to an abrupt halt, staring at him.

Clayburn was so tired it took him a moment to understand why. He walked past her into the barn and pulled on his Levi's, buckling the belt loosely around his waist. Velma had followed him, and she stood there watching him—until she remembered the cloth in her hand and came over to wad it into a bandage against his wound. As she tied it in place she asked, "Where're Jace and Greco?"

He told her, and then said, "I can smell it. Where is it?"

"Up in the hayloft. I figure you might want to stretch out and catch up on your sleep after—"

"I do." Clayburn climbed the ladder to the loft and found a tray on the floorboards next to a mound of hay. Velma had taken him at his word. There was a glass and a pitcher full of milk, and a plate heaped with hot ham and six fried eggs. He settled down in the hay and started on the meal, not hurrying it, eating slowly and savoring it.

Velma came up the ladder and stood there, watching him eat. After a time she said in an unsteady voice, "I was real worried about you, Clay."

"So was I," he said, and between mouthfuls he told her what he wanted her to do when she got back to town.

She listened without comment until he finished the meal and stretched out on his back with a contented sigh. Then she asked him, quietly, "Ready to pass out?"

"I'm tired enough." He locked his hands behind his head and looked up at her. "But I've been holding myself in tight so long it'll take awhile to finish unwinding."

Her lips curved in a slow smile. She knelt beside him and looked closely into his eyes. "If it's unwinding you need—I could help some."

His hand reached up and took hold of the back of her neck, his long fingers tangling in the silken richness of her hair. "Yes," he agreed, "you could."

She sank down into the hay with him and proceeded to do so.

He was sound asleep when she left him. As she mounted her horse and rode out down the pass, she decided that the first thing she would have to do when she reached town was make herself a pot of strong coffee. The trouble with putting a man to sleep like that was it left her feeling lazily drowsy herself. And she was going to have to stay awake. Wide awake. It was going to be a long night.

When Greco and Harcourt rode back into Niles' barn they found Clayburn sitting up on the driver's box of the stagecoach, having a smoke and waiting for them.

"It's done?" he asked as he climbed down.

"It went perfect," Harcourt told him, with the excitement of it tightening his voice. "There was a light on in the main room of that ranchhouse Wheelock took over, and we began pouring shots in through the windows from up on the hill. You never saw a light go out that fast. We scared hell out of them."

"They head for Glory Hole?"

"Two of 'em did," Greco put in drily as he and the deputy dismounted to give their horses a breather. "One of 'em made the mistake of opening the side door and trying a couple shots back at us. Harcourt here put a bullet through his leg. Guess that one's still holed up inside. The other two got out a back window to their horses and lit out, fast."

Clayburn looked at Harcourt again. "Sounds like you enjoyed yourself."

"I liked it fine," the deputy stated flatly.

Greco grinned at him fondly and then looked to Clayburn. "Don't worry about our deputy, Clay. He'll do."

"I guess he will." Clayburn dropped the glowing stub of his cigaret, ground it out, and went to saddle the big gray.

Greco got a spare Colt from his saddlebags and stuck it down inside his belt, to be used when the one in his holster ran out of ammunition and there was no time for reloading. "Gonna be a big night," he said happily to no one in particular. He looked about ten years younger than he was as he said it.

The three of them rode out of the barn together, heading down the pass toward Glory Hole.

Velma was waiting for them half a mile north of the town. She wasted no time before getting down to essential information as they pulled over beside her: "Wheelock just left town heading for his ranch—with six of his men. That leaves Torrey and ten more still in Glory Hole. And that's still bad odds, Clay."

But Clayburn was scowling at something else. "Wheelock rode out, too?" He'd been hoping they'd have a chance to nail Wheelock early in the game that night. With Wheelock taken care of, the rest of his hired guns would have faded away to other places, other jobs.

"What the hell's it matter?" Harcourt said eagerly. "He'll be back."

Clayburn looked at him. "Sure he will. Along with all the rest of his gunhawks, and knowing what he's riding into—if anybody slips out of town and gets the word to him."

Greco gave a short laugh. "We don't even know if we'll still be alive when Wheelock shows up. So what's the use thinking ahead that far? From what I've heard about this character Torrey, he's pure murder with a gun. And the other ten he's got with him in town ain't exactly amateurs, either."

Velma broke in with another piece of information: "I ran into Rowse, Dixon's foreman, when I was riding out this way. He was going through town on his way down to Morgansville to send a telegram to the sheriff."

Clayburn turned to her. "They found the cattle we put Wheelock's brand on?"

"Yeah. So you *could* wait till the sheriff gets here before . . ."

Clayburn shook his head. "Too long to wait. Wheelock'd have all his men back in one bunch by then, too many for the sheriff and us put together. Right now we've got Wheelock's crew split three ways. So it'll have to be now."

"Then let's get it started," Greco drawled, and turned his horse back into the pass.

They stayed together until they were just outside Glory Hole. There the three men drew up while Velma cut away from them, circling to enter the town from another direction. There was no need to give her last-minute instructions. She knew her part in what was coming.

When she had vanished among the buildings, Clayburn looked at Harcourt and said, "All right, Deputy, just remember not to get careless. We're gonna try to take 'em a little bit at a time, but that'll be finished the second one of them spots us doing it. And we can be caught at it any time from here in. So watch every window and door . . ."

"Along with every rooftop," Greco added wryly. "Also every alley and the shadows along the boardwalks."

"I know all that already," Harcourt snapped impatiently. "Let's go!"

They went. They entered the town riding as far apart as the width of the streets would allow—Greco leading the way up the left-hand side of the street, Clayburn following 15 yards behind riding the middle of the street, and Harcourt bringing up the rear along the right-hand side of the street. Each of them eyeing the dark alleys, windows, doorways, roofs.

They neared the central plaza of the town and circled around behind it to avoid crossing that much lighted open space. When they were in sight of the back of the jailhouse, they dismounted and hitched their horses to a rail.

Harcourt turned suddenly to Clayburn and whispered, "I want to handle this part."

Clayburn frowned at him. "We already decided Greco would—"

"I want it," the deputy repeated quietly.

Clayburn quirked an eyebrow at Greco, who nodded. "All right. But remember—neat and quiet."

They started up the alley beside the jail, leaving their carbines in their saddle boots. When they reached the other end, Greco and Clayburn stopped. Harcourt turned the corner alone, walked to the open front door of the jail, and went in.

One of Wheelock's gunmen was in charge in the small office, slouched in a chair with his feet up on the desk, his fingers laced together across his middle. He turned his head as Harcourt started across the small room toward him, saying his piece automatically before he saw who it was: "Just leave your guns on the rack over th——" Then he recognized Harcourt, and a big grin spread across his face. "Well, well, if it ain't the deputy. Come to see how we're taking care of your little—"

Harcourt had reached him by then. He snatched the gun from his holster before the gunman realized what he was doing, and slammed it full-force across the gunman's temple.

The man went over backwards and crashed to the floor, chair and all.

Clayburn stepped in through the doorway and looked down at the gunman's unconscious face. "Well—that was neat enough. A little noisy, though."

"It felt good," Harcourt said softly. "*Real* good." He holstered his gun, took the deputy's tin star from his pocket, and pinned it on his shirt where it belonged. There was a coldness in his face that was new. He didn't look very young any more.

It was odd the way work like this affected different men, Clayburn thought; the way it was aging Harcourt, and giving Greco back his youth.

He pulled off the unconscious man's gunbelt and tossed it toward the gunrack while Harcourt opened a desk drawer and got out four pairs of handcuffs—the entire supply. He stuffed them into his pockets, and then helped Clayburn carry the gunman's heavy figure to the door. They went through it swiftly, not stopping until they were around the corner and into the dark alley beside the jail.

Greco was leaning against the corner of the alley, appearing to be relaxing there while his eyes kept up a constant scanning of the open square. He backed into the alley after them and looked at what they were carrying with open pleasure. "One down. Ten to go."

A short distance behind the jail there was a small adobe building that had once been a boot-and-saddle shop, before being abandoned some weeks back by an owner, who'd decided to leave town rather than pay Wheelock protection money. Greco kicked open the sagging plank door and they dragged the unconscious gunman into the dark interior. He was left there on the floor, with his arms handcuffed around a heavy counter post.

Leaving the small building, the three of them went to their horses and got their carbines. Then they made their way cautiously through a series of dark alleys in the direction of Wheelock's headquarters, checking carefully before crossing any open lighted space to make sure there was no one around to see them. They had one advantage working for them now: there were only three hours left until dawn, and there was hardly anyone out on the streets. The townspeople were asleep, and most of the travelers and visitors to the town were bedding down by now as even the saloons and red-lights prepared to close up for the night.

About a block from Wheelock's headquarters, Clayburn slid his carbine out of sight under a boardwalk. They moved on until they reached the corral behind the stable next to Wheelock's building. Harcourt left his carbine on the ground against the base of the corral's low adobe wall, where the night shadow would hide it. A block farther on Greco hid his carbine behind some trash boxes in an alley.

This was standard procedure for any experienced town lawman: you always stashed some extra weapons around the area where there was likely to be the most trouble, just in case you needed to put your hands on one in a hurry. You might never need it. But when you did, it could make the difference between living and dying.

Having taken care of this rudimentary precaution, they circled back to the rear of the jail. They waited there only a few minutes before Velma appeared, out of breath from running.

"There's one checking the red-lights down at the other end of Front Street," she told Clayburn. "And another one coming down Plummer Street toward the square. They're the only ones I've seen out on the streets. If you want me to look some more—"

"No. Go keep an eye on Wheelock's place now."

As she hurried away the three men turned in the opposite direction and began making their way through back alleys toward Plummer Street.

The gunman strolling down Plummer Street was making a last inspection before reporting to Torrey and calling it quits for the night. He was nearing the intersection of Plummer and Trail Streets when a man came out of Trail Street up ahead of him. The man was momentarily caught in the light from a saloon. Then he turned the corner and started off in the opposite direction, walking away up a shadowed boardwalk past a row of dark stores closed for the night.

The gunman didn't know Clayburn, but he caught a glimpse of the gun Clayburn was wearing as he turned the corner. Abruptly, he quickened his pace, hurrying across the intersection and up onto the shadowed boardwalk after Clayburn. "Hey—you!"

Clayburn stopped and turned back toward the gunman. "Me?"

The gunman marched up to him and snapped, "What're you doing, wearing a gun inside town limits?"

Clayburn stared at him stupidly. "I just rode in. Ain't guns allowed in this town?"

"Can't you read? There's signs all over the place saying you got to check your weapons at the jail till you ride out."

"Okay—don't get so sore about it." Clayburn unbuckled his gunbelt and let it dangle from his hand. "Where's this jail I'm suppose to leave it at?"

"Down that way." The gunman started to turn and point toward Water Street. "You cut left when you—"

Clayburn swung the gunbelt like a whip, lashing it at the other man's face. The holstered Colt caught the gunman squarely between the eyes, toppling him sideways against the hitchrail. He sagged against the rail, stunned but not quite out, fumbling weakly for his own gun. Clayburn whipped the gunbelt up, over and down. The holstered Colt smacked across the back of the gunman's head. The man's arms dropped and he slid down off the hitchrail, settling into a limp heap at Clayburn's feet.

Harcourt came out of an alley behind Clayburn and hurried over to help him drag the unconscious gunman back into the alley. A moment after they vanished into its darkness, Greco stepped from the mouth of another alley on the other side of the street and strolled across after them. He kept up a constant surveillance of the surrounding buildings as he moved. By the time he reached Clayburn and Harcourt, they had the unconscious gunman's arms across their shoulders and were heading back toward the rear of the jailhouse. They walked with the limp figure hanging between them, his toes dragging in the dust. Greco took a last look at Trail Street and then followed some distance behind them, studying each dark window and shadowed recess where someone might be hidden, watching them.

They got the second gunman into the abandoned shop

behind the jail and handcuffed him to the post beside the first one. Then they started out again. Harcourt, walking between Clayburn and Greco, knew that if he lived through this night he would never be quite the same again. The way they were slicing away the opposition's superior odds made him feel like part of a methodically efficient three-man machine. It gave him a heady sense of power he had never known before. Yet he knew, as well as the other two, that part of it depended on luck. And he remembered one thing Clayburn had warned him about: that luck could be stretched just so far before it snapped.

Some minutes later one of Wheelock's gunmen stepped out of a red-light house and paused on the wooden sidewalk to light a cigaret. He shook out the match and strolled on toward the next building. As he approached an alley he automatically dropped his right hand to his holstered gun and slowed his pace. He was almost to the alley when a man emerged from a dark doorway on the other side of the street and started across toward him.

The gunman turned to face him, his fingers closing around the grip of his holstered gun. The first thing he noticed about the approaching man was that he was wearing a gun. Then he saw the glint of the tin star on the man's shirt. And then the man was close enough for him to see it was Deputy Jace Harcourt.

Harcourt reached him and said quietly, "You're wearing a gun in town."

The gunman took the cigaret from his mouth with his left hand and looked at the deputy insolently. "So?"

"So you're under arrest."

The gunman almost laughed. "What?"

Greco stepped out of the alley behind him and said, "You heard him." And slammed a clubbed Colt across the back of his skull, just behind the ear.

The gunman's legs buckled and he sagged forward into Harcourt's waiting arms. Harcourt immediately dragged his limp form past Greco into the darkness of the alley. Greco stayed where he was, carefully scanning the line of buildings across the street.

On the other side of the street, Clayburn stood in the

shadowed doorway from which Harcourt had appeared, studying the windows and doorways on either side of the alley where Greco waited. When he was as sure as it was possible to be that no one on that side had witnessed what had happened, he started across the street toward the alley beside Greco.

He had reached the middle of the street when Greco twisted to his right and whipped up his Colt. He fired it a split-second before a gun roared from a second-floor window of one of the red-light houses behind Clayburn. A man's cry of agony rang out as a bullet whispered past Clayburn's head and chopped the dirt of the street in front of him.

Greco fired again as Clayburn spun around, drawing his gun as he dropped to one knee. He saw a man topple forward out of the upstairs window. A gun spilled out of the man's hand as he crashed headfirst to the roof of the boardwalk under the window, rolled off it, and fell to the street below.

A woman began screaming at the top of her lungs inside the building. Lights went on inside windows as the shouts of other women sounded. Clayburn rose up off his knee, keeping his eyes on the building as he backed toward Greco.

They were all through getting free cuts at the opposition. Their luck had stretched as far as it was going to—and snapped.

13

VELMA WAS CROUCHED down in the shadows against the side of a building almost directly across the street from Wheelock's headquarters when she heard the footsteps behind her. She twisted around, a stab of fear going through her before she saw Clayburn coming up through the shadows, followed by Greco and Harcourt.

She rose to her feet as they reached her. "One of Wheelock's gunfighters went running into the saloon over there a minute ago. Augie, they call him. He came right back out—with Torrey, Sims and Yarborough. They headed that way—turned into Water Street."

Greco squinted reflectively toward the saloon across the street. "Means they left some behind in there—but not more than three."

"Three against three," Harcourt whispered eagerly. "Let's bust in before—"

"There's usually one up at the top of the stairs," Clayburn cut in. "That's too good a position. Come in as soon as you hear me take him." He touched Harcourt. "You concentrate on the bartender, nobody else. There's a shotgun behind that bar." He looked at Velma. "Get back to your place and stay put. Don't come out again, no matter what."

"Are you sure there's nothing else I—"

"Get *going!* We haven't got much time before Torrey and the rest head back this way."

Velma hurried away along the wall of the building. Clayburn waited until she was gone. Then he started across the street, angling away from Wheelock's saloon. Greco and Harcourt stayed where they were, watching him disappear inside the livery stable next to the saloon.

Less than a minute later the figure of Clayburn reappeared, up on the roof of the livery stable.

Clayburn moved across the roof in a crouch, his Colt gripped in his right hand and his other hand trailing a big, thick burlap grain bag. When he reached the edge of the roof he paused and looked down across the alley at the window of Wheelock's second-floor office.

The window was closed. The room inside was utterly dark, which meant the door must be closed. That would give him a small but vital extra bit of time.

Wrapping the heavy burlap around his torso and head, he poised himself on the edge of the roof, gauged the distance across and down. Then he launched himself into space, jumping feetfirst across the alley, pulling the burlap across his face as he hurtled downward at an angle. His boots smashed into the window and the rest of him crashed through after them, the burlap protecting his face and hands from the flying slivers of glass.

He struck the floor inside with his left hip and shoulder, the impact knocking the wind out of him and his forward momentum somersaulting him and ramming him against the edge of the desk. He was clawing the burlap away from him and trying to suck air back into his lungs when the office door was flung open—and the figure of a man with a carbine in his hands was starkly outlined in the doorway by the light from the saloon behind him.

The man was still trying to see someone inside the dark room to fire at when Clayburn shot him. He aimed dead-center on the starkly outlined target and hit the Colt's hammer twice in rapid succession with the heel of his left hand, the double roar booming deafeningly within the confines of the small room.

Both bullets got the man in the chest and hurled him backwards out of the doorway. His back collided with the bannister next to the top of the stairs and he went over it, crashing to the saloon floor below. There were only three other men in the saloon—the bartender and two gunmen. The bartender grabbed for the sawed-off shotgun as the other two spun toward the rear of the saloon, their eyes and their guns tilting upward toward the open door of Wheelock's office.

That was when Greco and Harcourt pushed in through the batwings behind them.

One of the gunmen spun back, trying to bring his Colt to bear on them. Greco's first bullet sliced his right eyebrow in half and drove on through the skull and into his brain.

The other gunman's reaction was just as fast, but smarter. He dived at a poker table, knocking it over and going down out of sight behind it.

The bartender was swinging the sawed-off shotgun around toward Harcourt and Greco when the deputy shot him in the chest. The bartender screamed and fell down behind the bar.

Greco was already hammering shot after shot into the overturned table, taking a step to his left with each shot. When the Colt clicked on an empty chamber he dropped it and snatched the spare gun from his belt. At the same time he reached out with his left hand, grabbed a chair, and threw it as hard as he could. The chair slammed against the overturned table and jarred it aside, exposing the gunman crouched down behind it. He had his gun aimed at the place where Greco had been when he'd started shooting.

It took the gunman a fraction of a second to shift his aim. In that fraction, Greco shot him. The slug got the gunman in the stomach as he squeezed his trigger. His bullet slashed past Greco's ear, and Greco fired again, finishing him.

By then the bartender had managed to drag himself to the other end of the bar, bleeding profusely but still clinging to the shotgun. Keeping down out of sight, he edged around the end of the bar, his finger sliding across the twin triggers. Clayburn stepped out of Wheelock's upstairs office and fired downwards, the bullet getting the bartender between the shoulder blades. The bartender's fingers squeezed both triggers as he fell face down on top of the shotgun. The double explosion lifted him clear of the floor and flopped him over on his back like a big smashed doll.

And then there was silence.

Harcourt's eyes went from the bartender to Clayburn. He looked a bit dazed as he turned to stare at the two dead gunmen, and then from them to Greco.

Greco grinned at him. "Still pretty fast for my age, ain't I?"

Torrey stood in the jailhouse office, looking from the overturned chair behind the desk to the empty cells. His face was calm and thoughtful as he turned to the other man in the office with him, a tall blond gunman named Augie.

"The girl in that red-light house was *sure* one of them was Jace Harcourt?"

Augie nodded. "She was sure. Said she didn't know the other two, but she got a good look at the third one and it was the deputy all right. Even saw his badge."

"The deputy and two other men," Torrey said softly to himself. "And maybe more she didn't see."

He looked again at the overturned chair, and then turned and left the room. Sims and Yarborough were standing watch out in front of the jail. Yarborough's face still looked as though someone had attacked it with a sledgehammer. His broken and swollen nose forced him to breathe with his mouth open, exposing the missing and broken teeth. Sims had lost weight and had the appearance of a man getting over a serious illness. He still wasn't able to eat much because his guts hurt from being clubbed across the stomach by Clayburn's carbine.

Augie was coming out of the jail behind Torrey when they heard the sound of the shooting begin, off beyond the other side of the plaza, at Wheelock's headquarters.

Torrey whipped the Colt from his holster and sprinted across the open square. Sims followed him, drawing both guns as he ran. Augie and Yarborough, each carrying a rifle, raced after them.

They were turning the corner into Front Street, with Wheelock's headquarters in sight ahead of them, when the last shots were fired inside it. By then they were close enough to be certain where the firing had come from.

Torrey had been in too many battles to need time now to figure out his strategy. There were a limited number of ways to get out of the building. In front there was the saloon entrance; and the mouth of the alley that ran between the building and the livery stable, under the window of Wheelock's office. In back there was the other end of the same alley, and three rear upstairs windows, one for each of the small bedrooms there. No back door or side doors.

Torrey motioned to Sims and Yarborough. "Get around behind the saloon." He snapped the order in a low, calm voice. "Stay down out of sight, watch the alley and the rear windows."

Sims and Yarborough raced off through the dark interior of the livery stable. As they vanished inside, Torrey motioned Augie toward the shadowed corner of a building where he could use his rifle on anyone trying to come out the front of the alley. Torrey himself backed into a dark doorway across the street from the saloon, holding the Colt loosely in his hand as he coolly divided his attention between the batwings and the mouth of the alley.

Inside the building, Greco and Harcourt reloaded their guns as they came up the stairs from the saloon. Clayburn holstered his Colt and stepped into Wheelock's dark office, picking up the carbine, which lay on the floor just inside. As Greco and Harcourt came in after him he pointed to the smashed window. "Drop down into the alley and get out the back of it. I'll cover you till you reach protection. Then you cover me."

They headed for the smashed window as he went out and opened the door to one of the rear bedrooms. It was a small room with two bunks, a chair and a bureau; and its single window was open. Clayburn closed the door behind him to keep the room dark, and crossed to the window in a crouch. Going down on one knee, he peered over the sill.

Off to the left of the rear of the building was the back of a restaurant. Directly across from Clayburn was the rear of a hardware store. No light showed from either building, and there was the dark mouth of a narrow alley between them. There was a small yard behind the hardware store, enclosed by a low wooden fence. A jumble of trash boxes and other junk cluttered the area in back of the restaurant. Below Clayburn's window was a scattering of empty barrels. Off to the right behind the livery stable was the corral with its low adobe wall, empty except for a freight wagon and several piles of full bags of grain.

Clayburn surveyed all this area out back carefully, and saw no one. Which did not necessarily mean no one was out there. The moon was hidden by the mountain crests now. There was only starlight to see by, and most of the area he was studying was shrouded in the dark shadows of the surrounding buildings.

Down between the saloon and the livery stable, Greco and Harcourt reached the rear end of the alley and paused, looking out into the same shrouded area behind Wheelock's headquarters. They saw no one out there, and knew that Clayburn would be firing by now if he had seen anyone. Greco drew a deep breath and charged out of the rear of the alley.

Two guns crashed out at him—one from inside the alley between the restaurant and the hardware store, the other from the cluttered pile of trash boxes behind the restaurant.

The same dark shadows that had hidden the two gunmen back there saved Greco from those first shots. He threw himself down and rolled across the dirt into deeper shadow. Clayburn tilted the carbine across the upstairs windowsill and began pumping shots into the alley between the restaurant and the hardware store. Harcourt went down on one knee by the rear corner of the saloon and blasted away with his Colt at the pile of trash boxes.

Their barrage, fired blindly at unseen targets, did what it was intended to. Yarborough dropped flat behind the trash boxes. He slithered to another vantage place among them, from which he would be able to fire with less chance of being hit by one of the deputy's bullets. Sims backed off hurriedly between the hardware store and the restaurant, to get away from the slugs whining in at him from Clayburn's carbine. And Greco was given time to crawl the rest of the way to the side fence of the hardware store's yard, getting out of sight behind it.

Clayburn went on firing the carbine until it was empty. He immediately dropped the carbine, drew his Colt, and went through the open window, falling feet first toward the ground. Yarborough sent one wild shot in his direction before he hit the ground and dropped to his knees behind a big beer barrel.

Harcourt fired one more shot at the trash boxes. Then the hammer of his Colt clicked on a spent cartridge. He began swiftly reloading while Clayburn fired around the barrel at the trash boxes. Greco vaulted the fence into the yard and started across it to get at Yarborough from the other side.

Out in front of the saloon, Torrey listened carefully to the sounds of the gunfire behind the building, hesitating while he watched the batwinged saloon door. No one came out of it, and after a moment longer, Torrey decided no one was going to. Briefly, he considered busting in through there. But it was too risky. He wasn't sure how many men Deputy Harcourt had with him. One of them might be down behind cover inside that saloon, waiting for someone to try coming in through the front doorway.

Finally, Torrey headed across the street toward the interior of the stable, motioning to Augie to take the alley.

Behind the hardware store, Greco crawled across the yard to the fence gate on the other side of it. He pushed the gate slightly open with his left hand. Holding the Colt ready in his right, he risked a fast peek through the opening into the alley from which Sims had fired. There was no one in the alley now. Sims was gone.

Greco frowned slightly and shot a look behind him at the rear door and window of the store. Nothing appeared to be moving inside there. But Greco pushed the gate farther open and crawled out, getting the fence between him and the rear of the store, just in case. Then he gave his full attention to the pile of trash boxes.

Clayburn, hunched down in the protection of the barrels behind the saloon, saw the fence gate open and read what it meant. He gave Greco three more seconds to get in position. Then he sprinted out from behind the barrels, heading for the low adobe wall siding the corral.

Yarborough's squat, hulking figure rose up from behind a trash box as he took aim with his rifle at Clayburn's running figure. Before he could get his sights lined up, Greco's gun roared from beside the yard fence. The bullet hammered into Yarborough's side, twisting him around. Staggering, spreading his feet wider apart to keep himself from going down, he tried to swing the rifle in Greco's direction. Greco's second slug caught him in the face, drove upward, and broke its way out of the top of his skull.

Over at the rear of the saloon, Harcourt had finished reloading and watched Clayburn reach the adobe wall in a low crouch. He was about to rise up off his knee to join him when he heard someone enter the alley behind him. The deputy twisted around and fired, at the same time that Augie's rifle boomed down the alley at him. The rifle slug slapped Harcourt's hat off his head. Harcourt's bullet broke Augie's left arm and spun him back out into the street, dropping the rifle as he fell in the dirt.

Augie let out a high-pitched scream as he rolled over on his broken arm. But his terror was stronger than his pain. Shoving up on his knees, he crawled along the edge of the boardwalk until he was where he couldn't be fired at from inside the alley. He knelt there for a second, panting, trying to clear the fog from his brain. Finally he decided the hell with it—it was time somebody headed out and took Wheelock word about what was happening in Glory Hole. Lurching to his feet, holding his dangling left arm to keep it from swinging, he headed up the street in search of a horse.

Behind the saloon, Harcourt hurried over to the low adobe wall and dropped to his knees behind Clayburn. "Now what?" he whispered.

There was no time for an answer. The rear door of the hardware store swung open and the two guns in Sims' fists blazed out from the darkness inside.

Sims might have been a good shot, but he was premature in giving his position away. He couldn't see Clayburn and Harcourt in the shadow of the wall. All he was doing was firing at their approximate position. One bullet chopped dirt up into Clayburn's face. The other thunked into the wall between him and the deputy.

Clayburn was instantly on the move again, sprinting straight ahead along the wall, keeping well down in its shadow. But Harcourt, behind him, decided it would be better to get the wall between him and Sims' guns. Rising off his knees, he started to vault over the low wall.

He was halfway across the top of it when Torrey fired from inside the livery stable. The bullet drove into Harcourt's right shoulder and smashed him off the wall. He struck the ground headfirst and sprawled out on his face, darkness engulfing his brain.

Clayburn did not pause to look back. He kept going in a crouch along the adobe wall, firing back at the dark rear doorway of the store as he ran. He was more than halfway down the length of the wall when his Colt clicked on a spent cartridge. He squeezed the trigger twice more, and the Colt clicked emptily both times.

The empty clicking was clearly audible to Sims inside the hardware store. And it didn't take any thought to realize what that sound meant. Sims came running out of the rear door, charging across the yard to get within point-blank range of Clayburn before he could reload.

Clayburn dropped the empty Colt and picked up the carbine they had stashed against the base of the wall there earlier that night. He tilted the barrel up and fired the carbine as Sims climbed over the fence toward him.

The bullet caught Sims just under the ribs and kicked him backward, dropping him down out of sight inside the yard. Sims groveled there, bent almost double and clutching his middle. Moaning, fighting against the blazing agony consuming his insides, he fumbled in the dirt with his right hand and found one of his fallen guns. He was forcing himself up onto his feet for a last dying try at Clayburn when Greco stepped out through the rear door of the store behind him and shot Sims in the back of the head.

Sims was still sliding down the inside of the fence when Torrey fired at Greco from inside the livery stable.

It was an impossible shot with a handgun, at that distance and at night. Even so, Torrey almost pulled it off. The slug punched a notch in Greco's right earlobe, and he leaped back, cursing, into the protection of the darkness inside the store. From there Greco began firing shot after shot into the rear of the livery stable, shifting aim slightly after each trigger-squeeze and spacing the bullets about a yard apart. He didn't expect to hit the unseen man inside there, just to keep him busy dodging—and give Clayburn his chance.

Clayburn took it, swinging low over the adobe wall and dropping down on his knees inside the corral. Torrey didn't waste a shot trying for him, because at that point Clayburn was far enough down the other end of the corral to have the freight wagon as a screen between him and the stable.

Rising up slightly against the wheel and side of the wagon, Clayburn edged to the other end of it. Beyond it was a short open space, and then a mound of full grain bags. He tilted himself slightly forward, tensing on bent legs. Then he dove for the mound.

Torrey fired twice, so fast that the shots almost sounded like one. The first slug ripped off the heel of Clayburn's left boot and the second thudded harmlessly into the bags of grain as Clayburn skid-landed behind them on his shoulder.

Clayburn drew in a deep breath. Exhaling slowly, he drew another. Then he got his knees under him. Being careful not to raise his head above the mound that protected him, he reached out with his left hand and separated two of the top bags of grain, just a bit. He slid the carbine into the groove this made, leaned into the mound, and sighted along the barrel into the dark-shadowed interior of the stable.

Then he waited. He couldn't see anybody to shoot at in there, yet. And Torrey couldn't get out the other end without being outlined by the light of the street. The next move was up to Greco.

Almost a minute went by before Greco reappeared. He came out of the alley between the store and the restaurant, where he could not be seen from the interior of the stable. And he carried a glass oil-lamp in each hand. As he neared the side of the corral he ducked down so the adobe wall would hide his movements. Reaching the wall, keeping down below it, he worked his way along until he was almost to the rear of the livery stable.

There he sat down on the ground at the base of the wall and took a box of matches from his pocket. Lighting both lamps, he turned their wicks all the way up until they were blazing with light. Then, without rising, he threw first one and then the other in a high arc over the top of the adobe wall and into the rear of the stable.

One of the lamps shattered in the middle of the stable, its

spreading oil aflame, casting a weird bluish glow. The other one smashed down on a patch of straw that blazed up immediately as the spilled, burning oil mixed with it.

Torrey was momentarily outlined by the flickering light as he leaped toward the protection of an empty stall. He never made it. Clayburn fired, levered, and fired again.

Torrey stumbled to a halt, his chin sinking down on his chest as though in thought. He turned slowly on one foot until he was facing Clayburn, and took a single faltering step toward him, the Colt still raised to fire in his right fist. Then he crumpled forward, face down across the licking flames.

It was over. At least, for the time being—until Wheelock came back.

14

WITH THE FIRST LIGHT of dawn the people of Glory Hole began venturing timidly out of their homes to find out what had happened. Singly and in pairs, and then in growing numbers as the news spread, they converged on the town's central plaza. To stare at what they found there in stunned disbelief at first, and then with a growing, contagious delight.

The three gunmen who'd been knocked cold one by one before the shooting had started were in the middle of the square. They were sitting on the ground, handcuffed to each other in a circle around the trunk of the big oak tree. Stretched out in a straight row to either side of the tree were Torrey and the rest of the dead ones.

Clayburn stood in front of the jail, watching the gathering crowd with knowing, cynical eyes. Greco was up on the roof of the tallest building in town, watching the most likely routes by which Wheelock might approach the town.

When Velma came out of the jail, Clayburn glanced at her and asked, "How's Harcourt?"

"Awful. Doc's arguing with him right now, trying to make him lay down."

"Tell that doctor," Clayburn snapped, "to mind his own business."

But at that moment Deputy Harcourt appeared from inside, his right shoulder and upper arm encased in bulky bandaging, his forearm held in a sling. Velma was right; he did look awful. His step was slow and heavy, his cheeks flushed, and his eyes feverish. His face was drawn taut with pain, and with a rigid refusal to knuckle under to the pain.

The doctor came out after him, complaining irritably.

"Dammit, Jace, you know you shouldn't be on your feet! You need to get in bed and stay—"

"I'll go to bed," Harcourt rasped. "Later—when I can."

The doctor had his mouth open to make his complaint a command. But something new in Harcourt's voice stopped him cold. He stared at Harcourt, closing his mouth slowly. Then he shook his head and stalked away without another word.

Harcourt turned to Clayburn and growled, "It would have to be my *right* shoulder. I can't shoot worth a damn with my left hand."

"You could with a sawed-off double-barreled shotgun," Clayburn said. "That's bound to knock over any target you point it at, close up."

"That's so." Harcourt considered the idea and liked it. He looked at Velma. "Go get me the sawed-off from Wheelock's saloon. Be good to have a spare handy. And an extra box of shotgun shells."

Velma blinked, surprised by the quiet command in his voice. Then she said, "Sure, Jace," and hurried off to carry out the errand for him.

Off in the middle of the square a townsman jeered at the trio of gunmen handcuffed around the tree. Another man laughed, and yet another took up the laughter.

"Listen to 'em!" Harcourt said bitterly. "They think it's funny now. A big joke."

"That's what we want," Clayburn told him flatly. "Why the hell d'you think we put Wheelock's men out there to be looked over? Once people start laughing at something, they can't ever be quite so scared of it again."

Harcourt shook his head slowly. "Laughing at unarmed men and dead men is one thing. It won't be the same when Wheelock—"

"They're laughing at Wheelock. Because they're seeing that Wheelock's men *can* be beaten and killed, like anybody else. That's something they didn't know before. They're ripe now, Deputy. Go talk to them."

"And say what?"

"Go tell 'em you're lifting the ban against carrying guns in town. Tell them they've got their town back. We've given it back to them, on a platter. It's up to *them* to keep it—if they want it."

"They want it," Harcourt said slowly. "But I don't know if they're willing to fight for it."

Clayburn smiled faintly and glanced again toward the crowd. "They don't know that either. They need a chance to find out. They're beginning to get the feel of having the town belong to them again. Let them get the feel of having guns in their hands again, too. Then see if they're willing to give that up, without a fight."

Dawn became morning, and Wheelock did not come. The morning drew on—and still Glory Hole waited, with growing tension.

It was an hour past noon when the farmer who was relieving Greco as lookout up on the roof of the hotel across the square lowered the pair of binoculars and called down to the jail: "Riders comin' south down the pass! Three of 'em! And a horse and buggy!"

Clayburn, lounging in a chair in front of the jail, came to his feet smoothly, a carbine in the crook of his arm. His glance swept the limits of the square, taking in the armed men waiting in the doorways and at the windows. They were too far away for him to see the expressions on their faces, and it wouldn't have done him any good if he could have. Their expressions wouldn't tell him whether they would hold or fold when the time came. Even they couldn't know that beforehand. With luck, maybe they wouldn't have to push too hard at the answer.

The lookout on the roof called down again: "Looks like old man Dixon in the buggy! And three of his cowhands!"

Clayburn's shoulders settled a little. From where he stood he could see straight up Plummer Street to the pass going north. Before long the horse and buggy appeared, coming into Plummer Street from the north, followed by the three horsemen. They came on down the entire length of the street, into the square. When they entered the square they paused, staring at the three men handcuffed around the tree, and the others laid out dead. Then they came on slowly toward the jail.

Dixon reined his horse to a halt and leaned forward a bit on the seat of the buggy, squinting at Clayburn. "What's been goin' on around here?"

"Deputy Harcourt's taken his town back from Wheelock," Clayburn told him.

"*Jace* Harcourt? And who else—you?"

"And a friend of mine. And Mrs. Lang."

Dixon stared at him. "Velma? She was—mixed up in that?" He jerked a thumb toward the tree in the middle of the square.

"Uh-huh."

Dixon frowned and rubbed his chin thoughtfully. "How's Cole Wheelock takin' all this?"

"We're waiting for him to come tell us that," Clayburn said without expression. "And what brings you to Glory Hole, Mr. Dixon?"

It came out slowly: "I'm here to wait for the sheriff. My foreman rode south last night to send him a telegram." Dixon hesitated, and then said the rest of it grudgingly: "Found out Wheelock's started puttin' his brand on my cattle."

"I told you," Clayburn said politely.

"You didn't have to tell me," Dixon growled. "I could feel it coming, myself. I just didn't want to . . ." He let it trail off, and looked past Clayburn at the jail door. "Where's Jace Harcourt?"

"Taking his turn at catching up on sleep. So's Mrs. Lang. We had a long night."

"And this friend of yours you mentioned?"

"At the other end of town, watching the approach from the south."

"I see." Dixon rubbed his chin again, and appeared to be struggling with something that was growing inside him.

Clayburn nudged it softly: "In the mood to join our little reception party? You—" he gestured at the three riders "—and your men?"

Dixon scowled at him for a time in silence. When he did speak, his voice was slow and careful. "My boys ain't gunhands. And I don't move around so good on those crutches."

"All they have to do is be able to shoot a rifle straight,

from a nice safe position behind an upstairs window." Clayburn grinned suddenly. "And for you, Mr. Dixon, we'd provide a nice comfortable chair you could sit in while you were doing it."

Dixon found himself beginning to grin back at him. He broke it off and scowled again, looking around the square at the men in the doorways and windows. His eyes came back to Clayburn. "Looks like you got just about the whole town carrying arms again. But will they *use* them, when the chips are down?"

"I don't know," Clayburn answered truthfully. "Will *you?*"

Dixon became silent again, thinking about it—but mostly studying Clayburn, sizing him up. At last he reached in back of him and pulled a rifle from behind the buggy seat.

"All right," he said. "We're in."

There was less than three hours to go before dusk when Velma, taking her turn as lookout on top of the hotel, called down: "Riders coming from the north! Looks like ten of them!"

Clayburn rose to his feet, opened the jail door, and called in through it: "Time for you to get up, Deputy."

Minutes later the ten mounted men came riding down Plummer Street, three abreast—with Cole Wheelock in front. As they approached the square, Clayburn saw that some of the men who'd been hunting him with Flood were riding behind Wheelock. But not all of them. And not Flood.

Clayburn thought about the approach from the other end of town—and about Greco waiting there, with Dixon's three cowhands and seven of the small ranchers and farmers.

Wheelock rode into the square and reined to a sudden halt, gazing blankly at what was in the middle of it. His nine men, spreading out behind him, looked also—at the three handcuffed gunmen, and all the dead ones.

The display had been calculated to make them think some long, practical thoughts. It obviously succeeded, from the nervous way some of them looked around them, and stiffened as they took in all the guns poking out of doorways and windows.

Clayburn was depending on the kind of men they were. Hired gunmen had no stake in any fight but their wages. When the risk in one place got to be more than the wages were worth, most of them preferred to drift on to other places, where the odds would be more heavily in their favor.

But whatever his men were thinking at that moment, Wheelock himself showed no response at all to what he saw in the square and around it. He kneed his horse forward toward the jail, and his nine men automatically spread out and followed him.

Wheelock reined to a stop several yards in front of the jail and sat there relaxed in his saddle, gazing down at Harcourt. He took in the deputy's bandaged right arm, the sawed-off shotgun tilted upward in his left hand, and the finger across the twin triggers. He also took in Harcourt's pale, drawn face, and the feverish look in his eyes.

Wheelock's glance slid away to rest on Clayburn, standing there with the carbine in the crook of his arm. "You," he said tonelessly.

"Uh-huh. Me."

Wheelock's eyes returned to Harcourt. "You've had yourself a big time, boy—you and your friends. How many friends you got, boy?"

"Just look around you," Harcourt said through his pain-clenched teeth. "Every damn man in this town's armed."

Wheelock laughed softly. "I see they are. But you don't know if even *one* of them's got the guts to squeeze a trigger against another armed man."

Clayburn knew this was true. He also knew that Wheelock couldn't be sure that the townsmen wouldn't fight—nor could his gunmen be sure. He said: "You're just talking, Wheelock. You're outgunned, and you know it."

Wheelock shrugged. "Most of those fools in those windows and doors can't even shoot straight. Every one of *my* men can."

"We outnumber you more than seven to one," Harcourt put in. "That makes up for it."

"I don't think so," Wheelock said. His eyes bored into

Harcourt's. "You made a mistake, boy, staying in this town. You've still got a chance to make up for it. Your last chance. Put down that shotgun, go for your horse, and ride off. Do it *now*."

"Go to hell," Harcourt told him evenly.

The tension in the square was reaching the snapping point, and when it snapped Clayburn wanted it to happen the right way. He suddenly took off his hat and said loudly: "You been saying our men won't shoot and can't shoot, Wheelock. I suggest your men watch this little demonstration before making up their minds about that."

He whirled the hat away from him. It floated across an empty space and settled down in the dust. The instant it touched the ground, a rifle cracked from an upper window of the hotel.

A bullet punched a neat round hole in the crown of the hat.

It had been fired by Dixon.

"That happened just because I tossed a hat away," Clayburn went on mockingly. "Guess what happens if any of you gunnies makes a wrong move. Maybe you're a fool, Wheelock. But maybe your men don't like the idea of dying for your foolishness. There's other places where they can earn their wages easier—and live to collect them."

Harcourt instantly took up the point, driving it home: "The sheriff's on his way here right now. Dixon sent for him—he's fed up with you, too, Wheelock. He's here in town, with his whole damn crew, ready to side with us against you." Without taking his fevered eyes from Wheelock, the deputy raised his voice and called out: "Ain't that so, Mr. Dixon?"

Dixon's voice came down clearly from the hotel window: "It sure is, Deputy."

Some of the gunmen who recognized the voice looked toward the window, and then at each other, liking the situation less and less.

Wheelock realized what was happening, and tried to turn it: "The sheriff's only one man. And he won't get here in time to—"

"That's true," Clayburn cut in with a malicious smile.

"By the time he gets here all your men'll be dead, if they try to buck this whole town."

"You men—" Harcourt said sharply, addressing himself to the mounted gunmen behind Wheelock. "—You've all committed enough crimes around here to get yourselves hung three times over. But you can ride away and none of us'll try to stop you. If you ride away *now.*"

Wheelock smiled thinly at the deputy. "You really think we're just going to turn around and ride off and leave this nice town of yours?"

"Your men are," Harcourt told him coldly. "Not you. *You're* under arrest for murder. You killed a marshal and hung a man in this town, remember? Now it's you that's gonna hang—after a strictly legal trial, though."

Wheelock's smile didn't change. His eyes remained fixed on Harcourt's. "This is just like last time, boy," he said tonelessly. "You remember the last time you stood there with that shotgun and threatened me. And you remember the way that turned out."

"Only this time," Harcourt pointed out, *"I've* got more guns than you."

"The rest of you," Clayburn said heavily, "just back off and be careful with your hands. There's nothing for you here anymore—and there's other places."

Wheelock had begun turning his horse slightly to the right and backing toward his men, his right hand hovering over his holstered gun as he began softly issuing an order: "Spread apart and—"

"Stay right there!" Harcourt cut in, tilting the muzzles slightly higher. This was it, the brink from which there was no turning back—the moment that could go either way. "Climb down off that horse and unbuckle your gun."

Wheelock went for his gun.

He was incredibly fast. He got the gun out of the holster and brought it up, and was swinging around to fire at Harcourt before the deputy finally squeezed the triggers.

The shotgun boomed and recoiled, nearly tearing itself out of Harcourt's hand. The concentrated double load of shot almost tore Wheelock's head off. He was slammed clear off the horse and dropped brokenly to the dirt on his back. There was nothing left of his face.

Clayburn already had his finger across the trigger of the carbine, ready to leap to one side and fire as he waited for Wheelock's gunmen to react.

For a moment the whole square seemed about to explode into violence.

And then the moment dissolved, and nothing happened.

Except that the mounted men looked down at what was left of Wheelock, looked at all the guns pointing at them from the surrounding doorways and windows—and settled back in their saddles, very carefully keeping their hands motionless.

The man who would have paid any of them who might survive a battle against overwhelming odds in this town was dead. So there was no point to risking their necks any further.

One of them looked at Deputy Harcourt and said flatly: "We won't give up our guns. Don't try to make us."

Harcourt was still staring, dazed, at Wheelock's body.

Clayburn spoke for him: "You can keep your guns. There'll be plenty of our guns watching you, all the way out of town. You got nothing to keep you here any longer."

"Clay!" Velma called down from the hotel roof. "There's six more of them riding in from the south!"

That would be Flood and his group. A shot inside town was obviously supposed to be the signal for them to close in from the other side. Clayburn watched the mounted gunmen with his eyes and his carbine. "Just sit back and wait this out," he told them in a voice as brittle as thin ice. "The first one of you that moves is likely to get hit by lead from five different directions at the same time."

Nobody moved. Clayburn thought of Greco and the others waiting back at the south end of town, wanting to be with them now, but knowing he had to stay put and help control this square.

Flood and the five with him didn't come into town to talk. They came—triggered by the signal shot from inside town, as prearranged—to smash at the south end of town violently and noisily; to create a diversion and throw the town into confusion, giving Wheelock and the rest of his men their chance to gain control of the central plaza. And then to sweep on to hit the rear of the jail and trap the deputy and whoever he had left with him inside the square.

They came fast, with guns in their hands, shooting out windows on either side of them as they swept into the street, ready to fire at anyone they saw out in the open.

The first one they saw was Greco; and they didn't see him in time.

Greco stood inside a shadowed doorway watching the six riders charging up the street toward him, firing at windows as they came. He thought of the ten hidden men waiting along this side of the street with him—seven homesteaders and three cowhands—and he knew it was touch and go whether they would stand and fight. He needed to do something, fast, that would throw them in the right direction.

When he suddenly stepped out from the doorway bringing up the Colt in his right hand, he did not aim at the riders. They made targets that were moving too fast, and he might miss. And if those riders came on unscathed through his first shots, it could scare the ten hidden men into holding their fire. So Greco triggered his first three shots, one right after the other, at the three lead horses.

Two horses went down and the third, nicked, swerved sideways and plunged up onto the opposite boardwalk before its rider could control it. One of the downed horses threw its rider head over heels across the middle of the street. The other pinned its rider under it, rolling over across his body.

The other mounted gunmen charged Greco, but did not reach him. The sight of the first two going down that easily achieved its purpose. Two shotguns boomed out from lower windows on Greco's side of the street, bowling over another pair of horses with their riders. From the upper windows eight rifles let go almost in unison, driving a down-slashing hail of lead into the two remaining riders and the dismounted gunmen.

Another horse went down. Yet another, riderless, wheeled around and went racing back out of town. Running men were knocked off their feet by the continuing hail of bullets. Men who tried to crawl to cover were nailed to the ground by a number of bullets pounding down into them at the same time. Greco shot a man trying to dodge into a doorway across the street, and then saw Flood going down flat behind a fallen horse. He twisted toward him and fired, tearing the hat from Flood's head. He squeezed the trigger again, and it clicked on an empty.

Greco dropped the empty gun and grabbed the spare one from his belt. He didn't quite manage to get it up when Flood slid his rifle across the body of the horse and fired.

The slug rammed Greco's chest. He stumbled backward two steps and leaned heavily against the side of the doorway. Through blurring vision he saw Flood scuttling away behind a horse trough toward an alley. Greco tried to bring the Colt up, but it had become too heavy to lift. He slid down the side of the doorway until he was sitting on the floor. Raising his left hand to his chest, he pulled it away and looked at all the blood on it.

Flood glanced back over his shoulder as he reached the alley, and saw that not a single one of the other five men who had hit the town with him was still on his feet. All the shots were being fired at him now. Flood dodged out of sight into the alley, ran the length of it and paused to listen.

The sound of firing behind him ceased. But that wasn't what he was listening for. He was listening for sounds of fighting from the direction of the town's central plaza.

And there were none.

No shots at all were being fired anymore, anywhere in the town. And this could mean only one thing, an incredible thing. Somehow, Wheelock had been taken—and the men with him had let him be taken. Flood considered all those town guns he and the other five had ridden into, and came pretty close to guessing what must have happened before they ever reached the town.

Flood moved on through the buildings and beyond them, getting into the timber beyond the town and heading west through the hills.

The nine mounted gunmen in the square still sat motionless in their saddles, ready to go for their weapons if it came to that, but not looking overly anxious for it to happen. They had tensed at the sound of gunfire from the south end of town, and they remained tense now that the firing had ceased. Clayburn kept his eyes on them and his finger across the carbine trigger, waiting.

A cowhand came running through the alley from behind the jail; one of the men who'd been stationed with Greco at the south edge of town. He jerked to a halt, staring at the nine mounted gunmen just sitting there. Then he looked to Clayburn and Harcourt, grinning.

"They came in shooting," he announced gleefully, "but it's all over now. We got every damn one of 'em!"

Clayburn watched the reaction of the mounted gunmen as this sank home to them. He gave it a moment to sink in deeper, and then told them negligently, "All right, now you can turn around and ride out the way you came in. Might be a good idea to keep on going, as far as you can and as fast as you can."

The gunmen began turning their mounts, one by one, eyeing the guns pointing their way as they headed back across the square. They were tensed to draw and fight if a single shot was fired at them.

But no shot was fired. Clayburn watched them ride north up Plummer Street toward the pass. He didn't think they'd be likely to double back later. There was nothing left for them here.

When the riders were out of earshot, the cowhand edged closer and said softly, "I didn't want to say it while they was listening, but one of 'em got away. Alex Flood. And he got that friend of yours on the way out. Bad."

Clayburn wheeled and raced around the jail, running all the way until he reached the south end of town and saw the knot of men up on the boardwalk, clustered around an open doorway.

He elbowed through them savagely and saw Greco sitting there leaning against the side of the doorway with his eyes closed. His legs sprawled out in front of him and his arms hung down limply, a gun still cradled in one hand. He was still breathing, but one look at his face told

Clayburn there was no use sending for the doctor.

He sat down on the plank flooring beside him. "Greco!"

Greco's eyes opened slowly, just a little. He squinted at Clayburn for some time before recognizing him. When he saw who it was he tried to grin.

"What the hell, Clay—it's a lot better'n dying—of old age—"

His eyes opened wider and then took on a fixed quality, still looking at Clayburn but no longer seeing him. He had stopped breathing.

15

CLAYBURN RODE OUT OF town and found Flood's tracks two hours before dusk. Flood was walking fast, taking long, swift strides, going west. It was obvious where he was headed. The nearest homesteader's place in that direction was a little ranch some ten miles west of the town. Flood intended to reach it after dark and steal himself a horse.

Clayburn angled west, kicking his mount to a hard run. He was alone. Some others had offered to come with him, but he had told them he didn't want them. This was a private thing now. He wanted no one else cutting into it.

He didn't follow Flood's trail directly. Instead he circled wide of the route Flood would be most likely to follow. Flood would be watching his back trail, alert for pursuit. Clayburn aimed to swing around in front of him.

He pushed the horse hard until he was five miles west of Glory Hole. Then he swung back toward the route Flood could be expected to take, and rode up onto the crest of a hill, into the shadow of a cottonwood tree. Raising a pair of field glasses to his eyes, he studied the country between him and the east, scanning it for sign of a man on foot coming this way.

He saw no one, but he went on looking, waiting. His reading of Flood's character told him Flood would come somewhere through this area. It was the shortest route to the nearest place where he could pick up a horse. Flood wouldn't be bothered much by the thought that a lot of riders might be pursuing him from town. He would trust his ability to spot them coming, from any direction, in time to shift course and give them the slip.

If they split up to hunt for him, that would be even more to Flood's advantage. It would mean he wouldn't have to hike the rest of the way to that little ranch to get mounted up. He'd be able to isolate one of the men hunting him—as Clayburn had done the previous day—kill him, and take his horse. He might be chased after that, but it would be dark before they could catch him. And they'd be able to trail him no farther through the night.

Clayburn continued to survey the country to the east through the field glasses. He scanned the long wall of the mesa to the right of him, the jutting mountain ridges to the left, and the wide expanse of rolling open country between.

In time a small figure came into the focus of his lenses, a man on foot, walking swiftly in his direction. Carrying a rifle.

Clayburn considered his next move. He couldn't charge at Flood on horseback in this open country without being spotted before he got within firing range. And Flood's rifle was accurate at a greater range than the carbine in Clayburn's saddle boot. He had to get near Flood before Flood could shoot. Which meant closing in on him through cover—the kind of cover that would make Flood's lack of a handgun a disadvantage, and where the easier maneuverability of a carbine would outweigh the greater firepower of a rifle.

Clayburn's mind worked with cold, clockwork precision as he studied the various bits of cover into which he might be able to lure Flood. He chose the one he wanted, some distance ahead of Flood: a small, dense growth of trees and bushes at one point along the base of the mesa wall. He gauged the distances, the speed at which Flood was moving, and the timing involved. Then he hung the field glasses from his saddle horn and started the horse down the slope, keeping it to a walk so that it wouldn't stir up much dust.

He rode across a long hollow to the base of another low hill. There he stopped and waited, continuing to keep careful check on the passage of minutes and seconds. When it was time, he rode the horse up the slope to the top of the hill. He looked down and off to his right at the stand of timber and bushes at the base of the mesa—and beyond it to Flood.

Flood was still well beyond rifle range, but much nearer to the cover Clayburn had selected than he'd been before. Near enough. Clayburn kicked the horse under him and raced down the slope in Flood's direction.

Flood reacted instantly, turning to his left and sprinting toward the small area of timber and bushes just ahead of him. Clayburn veered and raced toward the other side of the timber. In seconds the trees were between Clayburn and Flood, forming a shield that hid each from the other. Clayburn reined up sharply as he reached his side of the timber, yanked his carbine from the saddle boot, and jumped down. He slapped the horse away from him in the opposite direction.

The horse ran until it was about three hundred yards away. Then it slowed down and began wandering aimlessly, head down, nibbling at grass. Clayburn went into the timber with the carbine in his left hand and his Colt in the right, every bit of instinct and training in him coming into play, his senses honed to sharp sensitivity, his nerves almost painfully keyed to react to any hint of danger.

Clayburn and Flood were both trapped there in that small area of cover now. Neither could leave it to reach the horse or go in any other direction in the open, without being helplessly exposed to a carefully-aimed killing shot from the one who remained in the protection of the timber. There was only one direction by which they could leave the trees and bushes: up—up among the jumble of rocks and boulders rising out of the timber and leaning against the lower half of the mesa wall. But no higher than that. Above the rock slide the rest of the cliff rose straight up. It could be climbed, but only very laboriously and slowly; and the man who tried it would be exposed all the way.

So neither of them could leave here—until the other was dead.

Inside the timber Clayburn put his back to a tree trunk and listened. His eyes searched the heavy clusters of bushes ahead of him and to either side. He heard nothing but a faint rustling, which he concentrated on for a time, until he identified it as the breeze stirring leaves in the upper branches of the trees; and nothing else. He saw nothing that he could identify as any part of Flood; but he had to be extra careful about counting on that. Dusk was beginning to close in. Outside the timber there was a good hour of daylight left. But down in here, under the thick overhanging foliage, everything was in murky, vision-obscuring twilight. It was difficult to distinguish the shadow of a man from the shadow of a bush, or a low-hanging branch.

He could go to ground, of course. Slide under some bushes and lie in waiting, hidden, for Flood to give away his position by making the first small sound. Flood had to be fairly close—to the left, the right, or straight ahead. But Flood might be playing the waiting game himself. If they both did that this duel could stretch on endlessly. And Clayburn wanted to get at him. There was no impatience in him, only a driving will to do what he had come here to do.

Clayburn eased around the tree trunk to the other side of it. He put down the carbine, holstered his Colt. Reaching up, he grasped the strongest lower branch and hauled himself up. He did it slowly and carefully, making no sound. When he was standing on the lower branch he reached up again and pulled himself onto a higher one. He stretched out there, under the protection of the higher foliage of the tree, studying the greater area he could now see below his perch.

He searched the shadows among the trees and bushes for a long time, but did not see Flood. Frowning slightly, he shifted position to climb back down.

A rifle cracked, from above him. A bullet ripped down through the leaves and twigs and impaled itself in the tree trunk, ten inches above Clayburn's position. He swung off the branch and dropped to the ground, grabbed his carbine, scuttled 15 feet to a spread of juniper, and slithered under it.

Hidden there, keeping his breathing slow and steady, he considered what had happened. Flood hadn't sprinted into the timber. He had immediately angled up into the jumble of rocks and boulders above, against the base of the cliff.

This did not surprise Clayburn. He had intended to search there next, after he had finecombed the timber. Flood had not been able to see him from up there. He had fired at the movement of the upper foliage caused by Clayburn's shift in position.

For a reason, of course. To let Clayburn know he was up there. So Clayburn would begin working his way up into the rocks. Not from this side of the timber, because Flood had already warned him he was directly above here. No—the way to get up would be to cross through the trees to the other side of the timber and try to work up from there.

So by now Flood was circling through the rocks toward the other side of the timber, coming down into it over there to lie in wait for him.

Clayburn pulled himself forward until his head was out from under the junipers. He looked around cautiously, then pulled the rest of himself out, and began creeping toward the other side of the timber. Not all the way, though. Only about halfway. Then he stopped and climbed another tree.

He stretched out on a solid upper branch and watched the area ahead of him under the trees and among the bushes, his eyes shifting from one spot to another, ceaselessly. He didn't see Flood, or any movement that might indicate Flood's presence over there. So he continued to wait, nothing about him moving except his eyes.

Several minutes passed. There was a flicker of shadow movement behind two saplings off to the left.

By the time Clayburn had the sights of his Colt lined up with the moving shadow it vanished, behind a tree stump. It did not reappear. There was a dead, rotting tree lying across the earth to the right of the stump, and spreading out behind this was a mass of bushes. Clayburn watched the bushes, but could detect no telltale movement among them. He watched a little longer, and then began climbing down the tree, keeping its trunk between him and the area containing the fallen tree and the bushes.

Flood lay under the bushes against the rotting remains of the fallen tree. He held himself motionless, hardly breathing, all of him concentrated in his sense of hearing. The other man would be coming this way soon, passing here to work his way up into the rocks. If the man made any sound in passing, the smallest kind of sound . . .

A twig snapped on the ground somewhere off to Flood's left, beyond his screen of bushes. Flood's head turned in that direction, his hands tightening on the rifle. It was odd, the twig breaking over there. Because if he had calculated correctly, the one he was waiting for should be coming from the opposite direction.

A similar sound came, from off to the left again. There could be no doubt about it this time: a twig snapping underfoot.

Flood got his elbows under him and started pulling himself under the screen of bushes toward the left.

Then he stopped himself.

He was certain who he was dealing with here. It could only be one person: the one who had almost killed him after he'd shot up the stagecoach—the man in black, the one he'd learned was called Clayburn. He remembered the macabre joke of the way his other rifle had been returned to him.

A man like that *might* accidentally step on a dry twig when he was stalking this close. But not twice.

So it was no accident. The other man was deliberately revealing his position, trying to lure Flood to it—into ambush.

Flood held himself still, peering in that direction, listening, trying to locate Clayburn's actual position over there. He was concentrating so hard on the area to his left that when a third twig snapped—this time almost directly behind him—Flood jerked around on the ground to look in back of him. His too-abrupt movement rustled some dry leaves under him.

A Colt revolver roared from very close behind him. A bullet ripped in through the bushes and slashed Flood's right hip. He clenched his teeth to keep from crying out in pain, and slithered away swiftly to the protection of the fallen tree. The Colt roared again, and a rotting chunk of wood was torn from the tree just above Flood's neck. He rolled quickly over the fallen tree, scuttled noisily through the next area of bushes, dropped to his stomach again, and snaked away silently along another course until he was behind the protection of a thick tree trunk.

There he crouched, teeth still clenched to keep from panting, ignoring his hurt and bleeding hip as he watched the area through which he'd come, ready to fire at the first sign of movement through it. There was none. And though from this position Flood could see quite clearly the place where Clayburn must have been when he'd fired those shots, he was not there now. That he must be somewhere very close was certain. But he remained invisible.

Flood experienced a faint queazy sensation in his guts that was so rare for him that he could not identify it for what it was: the beginning of panic. He fought it down, and decided the rocks above made a safer position for him. Having gained it first, he should never have left it.

Turning, he began working his way back up among them, keeping well down between some boulders as he left the trees, going down on his knees and crawling as he got higher above the timber.

When he was halfway up to where the rock slide ended and the sheer wall of the mesa cliff began, he stopped and backed into a crevice. There, protected on both sides by juttings of stone and holding the rifle ready, he watched all he could see of the rocks below, waiting for Clayburn to come up toward him.

Time passed, and no one came. He listened continually for the faintest sound, but heard nothing. Finally, Flood began studying the area of timber below again. He studied it from one side to the other, slowly and with concentration. But there was no movement there other than the stirring of the upper foliage in the breeze.

Flood licked his lips and gazed beyond the timber, at the open, rolling land surrounding it—at the saddled horse grazing out there. If he could go back down into the timber and race out and reach that horse . . . But he knew he couldn't. He would be dead before he got halfway across the open space to the horse.

Flood put aside the thought and returned his attention to the rocks below and around him. Dusk was beginning to close in, changing and lengthening the shapes of the shadows cast by the rocks and boulders, making it difficult to be certain if a shadow showed where there shouldn't be one.

Bootleather scraped against stone off to his right. Flood turned without sound in that direction, bringing up the rifle a bit, his lips thinning back from his teeth as his finger slid across the trigger.

The sound wasn't repeated. Flood watched and listened, waiting. There was no way Clayburn could get past him on the right there without exposing himself for one fatal second. He waited patiently, like a wolf ready to strike at a trapped rabbit.

His waiting had stretched to more than ten minutes when he heard bootleather scrape stone again—but this time off to his *left*. Flood spun around toward the sound, his heart suddenly beating wildly, the peculiar queazy sensation coming again. There was no one in sight over there, either. Flood began to get the feeling that he was being toyed with, taunted.

Anger filled him, dispelling the other feelings. His narrow face hardened, and his hooded eyes slitted. There was one answer to the game Clayburn was playing to get at his nerves. The answer was to go higher up among the rocks. As high as it was possible to get. And there to wait, where Clayburn could not possibly get around behind him.

Flood got his feet under him and began working his way upward, moving silently, picking his route with infinite care. He was almost to the top when there was a sound behind him. It was a very small sound. Few would have heard it. But Flood did, and he spun around and fired the rifle as he finished the spin.

Clayburn was just stepping out from behind a boulder there when Flood made the turn. He had already checked himself in midstep and started to pull back on seeing Flood, but even so the slug almost got him. It slammed off the side of the boulder in front of him, slashing chips of sharp-edged stone at his face, making him twist away as he made the backward step.

His heel came down on loose stones, and they rolled under the heel as he twisted, throwing him off balance. He slipped off the ledge he had been climbing, and toppled straight down some five feet, falling on top of a boulder.

He landed awkwardly and heavily, the knuckles of his right fist cracking down hard against the surface of the boulder. The impact numbed the whole hand momentarily, and his Colt was knocked out of its grasp—clattering away down through the rocks below.

Clayburn rolled swiftly in the other direction, falling into a space between the boulder and the cliff itself, under a jutting overhang. He was safe from Flood's rifle there, for the moment. And as he opened and closed the fingers of his right hand the numbness began to leave it. But the Colt was gone, and he couldn't get it back without exposing himself. He was left with only the carbine gripped in his left hand. And, of course, the knife sheathed inside his left sleeve.

Clayburn got his knees under him and his finger across the carbine's trigger. He inched forward toward where the protecting overhang ended. Reaching the end he paused, stretched out, and then darted his head and the carbine out past the overhang, ready to fire upward at Flood.

But he jerked back instantly on seeing Flood up there, at the top of the rock slide, aiming the rifle down at his exact position. The rifle cracked in the same instant, the bullet flashing through the place where Clayburn's head had been, slapping against the side of the boulder, whining off it at an angle.

For a moment, Clayburn remained motionless under the protection of the overhang. Then he pushed the barrel of the carbine out beyond it again, being careful this time not to expose his head. The appearance of the carbine barrel did not draw Flood's fire. There was only a waiting silence.

Resting the carbine on rock, Clayburn stayed the way he was for a time, considering the situation. He pushed the carbine out into the open a little farther. But still Flood did not fire at it.

Clayburn realized he could get out from under the overhang by backing out the other way. But though that way out would hide him from Flood's rifle fire, it would not get him to Flood. Because up there where Flood was now, there was no way to get around behind him.

Clayburn drew the carbine back a few inches and gave the situation some further thought.

Up at the highest point among the rocks, Flood kept his eyes on the spot where the carbine had just been drawn back out of sight, and waited for Clayburn to expose himself again. But minutes went by, and Clayburn did not appear for another try at him. Frowning, Flood edged over to his left, his back still against the cliff, until he could see the barrel of Clayburn's carbine again. If he could have edged further in that direction, he could finally reach a point from which he could see Clayburn, as well as the carbine he was holding. And then it would be all over. Unfortunately, there was no way he could get any farther to the left. So he stayed where he was, watching what he could see of the carbine barrel, waiting for Clayburn to make the next move.

Clayburn made no move. Minutes dragged by. It was getting murkier. And with the coming of darkness, Clayburn would be able to work his way up toward him with some safety. Flood considered this for a moment. He looked away, across the top of the timber and the clearing—toward the horse wandering out there. Then he looked at the carbine barrel again. And came to a decision.

Clayburn was obviously trying to outwait him now. But there was a risk in that, too, when the other man knew your position. Flood rose up, just a little. Without making the slightest sound, he began working his way downward, keeping the carbine's muzzle in view every second, ready to drop down out of sight the instant it began to move.

Finally, Flood reached the place he'd been working toward. Going down on his knees, he began crawling silently over the top of the overhang that sheltered Clayburn. When he was at a point directly above Clayburn, he leaned forward, holding his rifle ready. He paused, braced himself on his knees, and tilted farther forward to fire at Clayburn's back below him.

But Clayburn wasn't there. There was only the carbine, left lying there by itself on the rock, jutting out past the overhang.

Instantly Flood understood: Clayburn had left the carbine there to lure him down to this spot, while Clayburn himself backed out from under the overhang, circled upward and . . .

Flood twisted around on his knees, whipping the rifle around and up.

Clayburn stood there on a ledge above him with his right arm raised back and his knife in the flat of his hand. His thumb held the hilt to his palm and the narrow blade lined up with his stiffly extended fingers, the point protruding several inches beyond their tips.

Flood had no time left for caution or thought. Clayburn watched his finger and sidestepped as it squeezed the trigger. The rifle boomed, its bullet lashing upwards, nicking the side of his belt in passing.

Clayburn leaned forward as Flood levered for another shot, and concentrated all his strength and skill into the throw. His right arm whipped forward and down, the knife flying from his hand. It flashed across the short intervening space, the sharp point going into Flood an inch under his breast bone. It drove in deep, the length of narrow steel blade penetrating almost to the hilt.

Flood's scream of agony became a dying sound as he toppled backward and fell from sight.

Clayburn climbed down onto the overhang and stepped to the edge. Flood lay below him on his back, spread-eagled across the humped top of the boulder, his eyes wide open and the hilt of the knife protruding obscenely from his middle.

Clayburn worked his way around the overhang and picked up the carbine with his left hand. He pulled the knife out of Flood's body, wiped it twice across Flood's chest, slid it back inside his sleeve, and started down through the timber to get the horse and ride away.